You Shouldn't Have To Say Good-bye

**Other Apple Paperbacks
you will enjoy:**

The Dollhouse Murders
    by Betty Ren Wright
Circle of Gold
    by Candy Dawson Boyd
Save the Loonies
    by Joyce Milton
Tough Luck Karen
    by Johanna Hurwitz
A Different Twist
    by Elizabeth Levy

You Shouldn't Have To Say Good-bye

by Patricia Hermes

AN
APPLE®
PAPERBACK

SCHOLASTIC INC.
New York Toronto London Auckland Sydney

ISBN 0-590-41355-4

Copyright © 1982 by Patricia Hermes. All rights reserved. Published by Scholastic Inc., 730 Broadway, New York, NY 10003, by arrangement with Harcourt Brace Jovanovich, Inc. APPLE PAPERBACKS is a registered trademark of Scholastic Inc.

12 11 10 9 8 7 6 5 4 3 2   8 9/8 0/9

For my children—and for Jessie

You Shouldn't Have To Say Good-bye

CHAPTER
One

✒ "WHEN YOU WERE a little kid, did you ever wish you could walk on the ceiling?" Robin had turned her head and was looking at me sideways, her huge eyes seeming even wider than usual, her dark hair streaming away from her face and down over the edge of the bed. We were both lying flat on our backs, and Robin stretched her legs and pointed her toes straight up. Perfect legs, rounded just right, not like mine. Sticks, I have. Thirteen-year-old sticks.

"Huh, Sarah, did you hear me?" Robin was still looking at me. "Did you ever want to walk on the ceiling?"

"Yup, still do. I imagine the whole house upside down, and I walk on the ceilings and pick my way over the light fixtures. Really wish I could do it."

"Yeah, me too." Robin bent her leg and examined her bare foot. "My toenails are gross."

"What's the matter with them?"

"I don't know. They're lumpy-looking."

"Poor baby," I answered. Perfect Robin, little doll-like face, huge eyes, thick, shiny hair, and a figure, small and curvy at the same time. I couldn't feel too sorry about her lumpy toenails.

"I mean it. They're really gross."

"Tough. Robin, you know you're pretty. What's it feel like?"

"What!"

"You heard me. You must know you're pretty. What does it feel like?"

"You know what?" Robin sat up and crossed her legs. "It's a pain. It really is. Only junior high, and the boys all bother me; and most of them are creeps. There are some boys I like, but they don't come near me. Sometimes I think they're scared."

"But it must feel good too, knowing everybody thinks you're cute. Doesn't it?"

"Yeah." Robin recrossed her legs, burying her feet with her lumpy toenails under her. She looked sad.

"What's the matter?"

"I don't know."

"Something."

"Yeah." She paused. "Did you know my mother was a runner-up for Miss America? Miss Arkansas, she was."

"Honest? I didn't know that!" I tried to picture Mrs. Harris, Robin's mother, but I couldn't. I just had this vague memory of a little woman at the end of the dark hallway at Robin's house, her hair twisted up in a towel, some kind of dark stuff on her skin. I had seen her only that once, because we hardly ever go to Robin's house. "So, why does that make you sad?" I asked. "You feel like you have to be Miss America too?"

"No!" Robin wriggled off the bed. "I'm bored. Let's do something."

"What?"

"Play with your hamster?"

2

"I'm tired of him."

"Ride bikes?"

I shook my head. "My bike's got a flat. Besides, I'm sick of bikes. There's no place to ride around here. Roller-skate?"

"Didn't bring my skates with me."

I made a face, but I didn't suggest that we walk over to Robin's house to get them, even though she lives only a few minutes away. It's just understood that nobody goes to Robin's house. "Pooh! What then?"

Robin just shrugged. She still looked sad, the way she gets sometimes, and I realized we had to do something or we'd end up staring at each other all afternoon. I knew my mom would have some ideas, or at least she'd give us a good laugh. I opened my bedroom door. "Ma!" I shouted.

Mom hates being called "Ma," and it's a joke between us. If I call her "Ma" she shouts back in an awful, superloud voice, "What?"

There was no answer, but I could hear the typewriter going in her downstairs office. I waited until she paused, then shouted again. "Ma!"

"What?" she shouted back, and I could tell by her voice that she was laughing.

"Ma, we're bored. What can we do?"

"Scrub the kitchen floor."

"Mommy, dearest, we don't want to scrub the kitchen floor. What can we do?"

"I have a whole list," she called back, "but I can't shout, so you'd better come down."

Robin grinned at me, and we both ran downstairs. My mom is a lawyer, and her office is on the first floor of our

3

house, with a side door for her clients. She set up her office at home after I was born so she wouldn't have to be away from me all day. She said she sure wasn't going to give up her work, the thing she loved most—besides Daddy and me, that is.

When we went into her office, she rolled her chair away from the typewriter and waved Robin and me into the big squashy chairs she has. "So"—she smiled at us— "you're bored, and yet you don't want to scrub the floor?"

"Nope." Robin smiled back at her, and as I watched, I smiled too. All my friends think my mom is neat, and it feels really good. Once, when we were little, we voted, and Mom was voted the best mom in the neighborhood. "Nope," Robin said. "I hate scrubbing floors."

"Smart girl," Mom said. She turned to me. "Ride bikes? Roller-skate?"

"You can do better than that," I said.

"Take your chicken for a walk? Dress up your dolls and put them in a carriage?"

"What?" Robin squealed.

"Imagine you're a grasshopper," Mom continued, and she began ticking things off on her fingers. "Paint a dog. Clean your toothbrush. Squeeze a turtle. Inspect your fingernails. Hold both elbows in one hand."

We were both giggling now, and Robin tried holding both elbows in one hand. She didn't do too well.

"Or make yourselves some Reuben sandwiches and take them out on the roof to eat."

"Really?" This time I squealed.

"Really. I bought all the stuff for Reuben sandwiches."

"Oh, Mom, you're wonderful!"

4

"I know." She smiled.

I love Reuben sandwiches. You make them with corned beef or pastrami and sauerkraut and cheese on rye bread and heat them in the oven until the cheese melts. Next to hot-fudge sundaes, they're about my favorite food in the whole world. "But can we really eat them on the roof?" I asked.

"If you're on the flat part over the garage—and if you don't tell everybody in the neighborhood and get me in trouble."

"I won't. I promise." I knew what Mom meant. She lets me do some things that other moms don't let their kids do. Sometimes the other kids try it, and then their moms get mad at my mom—like the time when I was little and Mom let me paint myself all over with watercolors. The other kids saw it and they tried it too, but they used house paint on themselves. It was a disaster, and the whole neighborhood was upset for a week.

"And you have to wear sneakers," Mom was saying. "No bare feet on the roof or you might slip."

"Oh, Mom, that's great," I said. Robin and I struggled up out of the stuffed chairs, and I went to Mom, wrapped my arms around her waist, and hugged her. "Thanks, Mom."

"*Ow!*" She sucked in her breath and pulled away from me suddenly.

"What's the matter? Did I hurt you?" I hadn't squeezed her that hard.

"Yes," Mom said quietly. She rubbed a spot low on her back and wiggled around, as if she were trying to get rid of a hurting place.

5

"I'm sorry," I said, puzzled.

"It's not your fault." Mom smiled at me, but she seemed puzzled too. "I've had lots of sore spots there lately, little things. I don't know why. Nothing, I guess." She smiled again. "Now careful with the sandwiches in the oven, and if you need help, shout. And don't forget the sneakers."

"Sneakers taste terrible on a Reuben sandwich," Robin said from the doorway.

Mom glanced at her, then burst out laughing. "Good girl!" she said.

I laughed too and looked at Robin. All the sadness was gone from her face.

Together, Robin and I turned to leave Mom's office, but as I closed the door, I looked back. She had rolled her chair back in front of the typewriter, and as I watched, she put one hand on that place on her back, a kind of puzzled look on her face again. But then she smiled. "Sneakers taste terrible on a Reuben sandwich." She laughed to herself.

CHAPTER
Two

✍ THE TROUBLE WITH Reuben sandwiches is that they take forever to prepare. It must have taken us an hour to assemble and heat them. Then we put our sneakers on and climbed out of the window of the spare bedroom and onto the garage roof. We settled down in a corner on the flat part near the section that goes up to the peak. It's a perfect place because you can see the street from there, but if you lean backward, toward the ridge, nobody can see you. We were halfway through our sandwiches when a tiny white car pulled up in front of the house and a fat man squeezed himself out. He waddled around the car to the sidewalk, staring up at the house as if he weren't quite sure he was in the right place. "Hi, mister!" Robin shouted. "Look up here . . ."

"Hush up!" I tugged at her arm, yanking her back out of sight. "That might be one of Mom's clients!" Mom gets mad if I'm not dignified when she has clients.

Robin stayed with me back out of sight, but she was giggling. "Gosh, is he fat! Probably ate too many Reuben sandwiches." She grinned. "Did you ever notice how fat people always have tiny cars? They look like they're wearing them."

7

I started to laugh. "Can you imagine what kind of car Julia is going to get when she grows up?"

Robin burst out laughing. Julia is a kid on our gymnastics team, and she's a good kid, but she's fat. She reminds me of the Pillsbury dough boy you see on TV. "A Volkswagen." Robin giggled. She sighed then and stuffed the rest of her sandwich into her mouth. When she had finished chewing, she said, "I'm bored. Let's do something."

"Robin! We're already *doing* something. You're a bird."

"Yeah, well, I'm restless." Suddenly, she began to smile. "I have an idea. I want to see what's going on in your mom's office." She lay on her stomach and started wriggling toward the edge of the roof.

"What are you doing?"

She looked back at me. "Going to lean over the edge and see if I can peek in the windows. See what Fat Man is doing."

"Robin, you're going to get me in trouble! Now cut it out."

She sighed again, but she crept back to me and sat up, cross-legged. "Okay," she said. "Boring, boring, boring." She looked around as though searching for something, then turned toward me, a little smile beginning to form again on her face.

"What?" I said. I knew something was coming.

"If your mother has a client, we can figure that they'll be busy for a while. Right?"

"Right," I said.

"Maybe even for hours. Right?"

"So?" I said.

"So-ooo." Robin was smiling. "See that peak up there?

8

I dare you to get up there and walk on it.'' She was pointing to the top of the roof, to the ridge that ran the length of the house. ''Bet you can't do it,'' she said.

''Bet I don't *want* to do it. That's crazy.''

''Then I'll do it.''

''Robin, no! You'll get killed.''

''Only if I fall,'' she said, grinning.

''Ro-*bin*!'' I tried to make my voice get the warning sound that Mom's does sometimes. ''Don't you dare!''

''I'm going.'' She scrambled away on all fours and began climbing the sloped roof to the ridge. She was moving really fast, and even if I could have grabbed her, I didn't dare for fear she'd fall.

''Robin, Robin, please stop! Please, you're going to get hurt. Dead.''

''You forget that I'm a robin, a bird. You said so yourself. And birds don't fall.''

''Funny,'' I said, hoping it sounded as sarcastic as I meant it. Robin was still scrambling up, and as I watched her climb, my heart began to pound with fear. At the same time I was just a little jealous. I would love to do that, but I'm way too scared.

''I'm supposed to have a pole,'' Robin called down to me. ''You know, like those people in the circus who walk the wires—the pole out for balance?''

''Then why don't you wait till you get one?'' I realized it was a stupid thing to say and that Robin would know that it was stupid too, but I would do anything, almost, to stop her. She gave me a weird look over her shoulder and finished climbing to the peak.

''Hey, this is something,'' she said after she had settled

9

herself up there. "You can see everything from up here— the church, even the school."

"So now that you've seen it, why don't you come down?"

She just grinned at me then, with what she calls her fiendish smile, and began inching herself to a standing position on the ridge of the roof. I watched her, fear making my throat so tight that I could barely swallow. She tottered a little, back and forth, her arms out for balance, but when she looked at me, she was grinning. "Well, here goes nothing," she said, but even though she was smiling, she didn't sound quite so sure of herself as she had before. And she was pale. Even from down below, I could see that, pale as a ghost.

"Robin?" I said softly. "Please?"

She either didn't hear or pretended not to hear, and she started off across the roof, one foot in front of the other. Left, right, left, arms out for balance. I couldn't watch. I closed my eyes and prayed. "Please, God, please. Even though she's a nut, she's my friend. Don't let her fall."

I opened my eyes a crack. She was still there, making her way to the far end of the roof, her back to me now so I could no longer see her face. "Please, God, just a few more steps?"

My prayers must have been answered because she was at the end of the roof. Slowly, she inched herself to a sitting position and swung around to face me. She took a deep breath and smiled, but then, instead of crawling back, now that she had done it, she began to stand up again, as though she were going to walk back.

"Robin!" I shouted. "You've already done it! You've proved it. Now cut it out."

She only grinned and began the trip back. Now that she was coming toward me, I could see the fear on her face. She was paler than I've ever seen anyone. She wasn't going to faint, was she? Again, I couldn't watch. I closed my eyes and swung around a little to face the street. And that's when I saw them—my mother and Fat Man, wide-eyed, clutching each other, staring up at the roof at Robin. I turned and looked back too. Robin had just completed the trip and she sank down behind me, creeping into a sitting position. "I did it! I did it!" She grabbed my shoulder.

I nodded, unable to speak, and Robin said it again. "I did . . ." Then I pointed to the street, to my mother, who looked as if she had just come alive and was rushing toward the house, raising one finger and shaking it at us. "I— did it," Robin said, with sort of a sinking tone.

"You sure did," I said.

CHAPTER
Three

🖎 THAT WAS SATURDAY afternoon, and I didn't see Robin or talk to her until Monday at school. Mom was so mad at me that I wasn't allowed to see *anybody* until Monday. She said that what we did was dangerous, and she called Robin's mom and told her about it, even though I cried and begged her not to. "I have to, for her own good," Mom said. Then, when Daddy returned from tennis that afternoon, I got the big lecture from him about how foolish I had been, even though I didn't do anything! Half of me was mad at Robin for getting me in trouble, and half of me was scared that she was in even more trouble. I couldn't wait till Monday morning to find out.

But even then, I didn't have much time to talk to Robin until gymnastics practice after school. We had been rehearsing for the gym show every day since school started, and that was the day we were to choose the events we wanted to be in. When I finally saw Robin, we were in the gym, getting ready for practice. She looked at me sheepishly. "Sorry," she said.

"Yeah, me too. Did you get into a lot of trouble?"

She just shrugged. "How about you?"

"I had to stay in all weekend. You know, I really

12

begged my mom not to call yours. But she said she had to.'' I tried to mimic Mom's voice: '' 'For Robin's own good,' she said.'' I made a face. "How much trouble did you get into?''

Again, Robin shrugged. "Not much. My mom—I don't think she even knew what your mom was talking about.'' She turned to the ropes. "Come on. Want to climb?''

She swung onto a rope, and I sat down on the mat and quickly pulled off my shoes. I was thinking about what Robin had just said about her mother. How come her mom didn't understand? What was wrong with her, anyway? But then Robin was yelling down to me. "Will you get your bod up here?''

I grinned at her and swung onto the rope, shimmying all the way up to the ceiling. At the top there's a huge metal rod that holds the ropes, and we're supposed to climb up, touch it, and then slide back down. Robin was on the rope next to mine, and we practiced a few times, going up and down as fast as we could. Once, when we got to the top, instead of just touching the bar, Robin swung off her rope and onto the rod, holding it as though she were chinning.

"You know better than that!" It was Mr. Anderson, the gym teacher, yelling up at us. "That's dangerous, and you know it.''

Robin quickly switched back to the ropes. "Sorry, Mr. Anderson,'' she called down, and she smiled at him.

But he didn't smile back. "You know the rules, Robin. If you do it again, you're out of the show. Period.''

"Yes, Mr. Anderson,'' she said meekly.

We watched him turn away, and Robin made a face

at his back. "Spoilsport," she whispered. She looked at me. "Everybody wants to spoil your fun. What routines are you going to do for the show?"

"Floor routines and the ropes. What about you?"

"Ropes and I'm not sure what else."

"Why don't you try the balance beam? You'd be great"—I grinned at her—"considering what you did on the roof on Saturday."

"Nah, too easy. Anyway, did you ever see the faces of the girls on the beam? Miss La-de-das. And besides, only the fattest girls choose the beam."

I giggled. "Yup, Julia."

I looked down.

Julia was on the balance beam just then, tottering back and forth, looking like a cow trying to walk a fence. She was wearing tight white shorts, but they were thin, and you could see her underwear through them, pink, with yellow flowers—tank-sized underwear. She got to the end of the beam then and swung around, one foot extended.

"Go, Julia!" Robin yelled.

Julia looked up and grinned, but as she did, she plopped off the beam and onto her rear end on the floor.

"O-kay, Julia!" Robin called.

Julia didn't look up.

"That wasn't nice," I told Robin. "Julia's a good kid."

"Yeah, but she doesn't mind. She knows I was just kidding her." She called down though, as if to make sure that Julia knew it was just a joke. "You okay?" she yelled.

Julia nodded, rolled her eyes, and rubbed her bottom, and we all laughed.

"Come on," I said to Robin. "Let's get down. My arms are killing me."

"Wait a minute," Robin said. "Why don't we work out a routine with the ropes? Something really spectacular, like maybe climbing up, switching ropes in midair, switching back. Something. Chin off the rod up there." With her head, she indicated the rod that Mr. Anderson had just shooed her off.

"You get on that, you get thrown out," I reminded her.

"Not if we don't do it till the night of the show, and by then it'll be too late to throw us out."

"But it's dangerous. He just said so. You know it's too fat to get a good grip on, and slippery, too."

Robin gave me one of those looks. "Don't be such a goody-goody."

"I'm not a goody-goody!"

"Well, whatever. A scaredy-cat then." Robin started to slide down the rope. "If you don't want to, I'll ask someone else. Robert. He won't be scared."

"I'm not scared!"

She grinned at me. "Then let's practice."

I made a face at her; then I grinned back. I knew I had just been had, but it was okay. For the next hour, we practiced hard, racing up and down the ropes as fast as we could, trying to switch ropes part way up, then switch back again. It was hard to do because we had to swing the ropes out to make them meet, then wrap our legs around each other's rope before switching over. Even though it was exhausting, it was fun. Mr. Anderson watched us for a while, then came to help us. He taught us how to heave

15

our bodies into the swing and how to hug the rope with our legs before switching. Of course, we didn't try to chin on the bar while he was there, and I hoped Robin would forget about that part of it.

When practice was finally over, Robin and Julia and I slowly walked home together. We were all pooped and we hardly spoke, just waved bye to one another at the corner.

When I got in, it was already almost dark. I opened the door and shouted, "Hi, Mom!"

There was no answer.

"Mom?" I went to her office door and listened, but there was no sound of voices and no typewriter. I knocked lightly, then opened the door. Sometimes Mom's using a tape recorder, or a dictaphone, or something with ear plugs, so she doesn't hear me call. But no Mom in her office.

"Hey, Mom?" I shouted.

"Honey? Sarah, is that you?"

I bounded up the stairs. "Hi, Mom."

"I'm in here, honey." Her voice came from the bedroom.

I went into her room and stopped, surprised. Mom's never in bed in the daytime! She was dressed, but lying down, and the blinds were drawn as though it were night. "What's the matter? You have a headache?"

"I don't know. I don't feel well at all." Mom struggled to a sitting position. She patted the bed beside her and I sat down, beginning to be worried. "I don't know what it is," Mom said when I sat down, and she sounded worried too. "I've talked to the doctor, though, and to Daddy.

Daddy's on his way home. As soon as he gets here, I'm going to the hospital.''

"The hospital! For a headache?'' My heart was thumping hard. "Why?''

"It's not a headache, Sarah. It's something else. See, there was blood today. And this soreness and ache in my back and side.'' She shifted uncomfortably in bed, then put a hand out to the quilt, trying to pull it up around her. "And I have a fever. I'm burning up and shivering at the same time.'' She didn't look at me.

I turned to the window, blinking fast, because I felt as though I were going to cry. I'm not a baby. I know mothers get sick. But I was scared.

"So what are they going to do at the hospital?'' I asked, still without looking at her.

"Don't know.'' Mom sighed. "But Dr. Kelly said we'd better run some tests immediately and find out what's wrong. That's why he wants me in the hospital, even though it's almost night.''

"But . . .'' I couldn't continue.

"Hey!'' Mom reached out and pulled me close. "Stop sounding so worried. It's going to be all right.''

"You sure?''

Mom smiled a little, then put on a fake frown and spoke in this really deep voice. "I—am—sure!'' She sounded like one of those voices you hear on TV, coming out of the sky.

I couldn't help smiling. "Really?''

She nodded, but she looked worried, and she sounded worried when she spoke again. "I hope so.'' She held me close. "Now, if you don't give me a love right this very minute, I'm going to get up out of this bed and beat you up."

I smiled into her shoulder and put my arms around her. I started to squeeze her hard, and then I remembered how I had hurt her Saturday. So I held her and hugged her gently, but what I really wanted was for her to hug *me*, to hold *me*, to tell me that everything was all right, because somehow, I was afraid it wasn't.

✍ IT WAS WEIRD, waking up the next morning with Daddy sitting on my bed instead of Mom. "Hey, Punkin," he said. "Wake up." He brushed my hair away from my face and kissed my ear. "Up and at it!"

"Go away," I muttered, rolling over and sticking my head under the pillow the way I usually do. I hate mornings, that day even more so, without Mom there.

"Come on." Daddy got off the bed then, and I could hear him pulling up the blinds. He started humming softly. "Morning has bro-ken . . ."

"Go away," I growled again. I couldn't imagine anybody singing in the morning. Even Mom knew that.

He went right on singing.

"Dad-*dy*!" I pulled the pillow tight around my ears, trying to shut him out.

"Come on, Punkin," he said again. "It's seven-thirty."

"What!" At that I sat straight up, pulling the sheet with me to keep covered. "Seven-thirty? Mom wakes me up at seven o'clock! I'm going to be late." I glared at him. He should know what time I wake up.

He just ruffled my hair and turned to the door. "Get dressed and don't be such a grouch. I'm taking you out

19

to breakfast, and then I'll drive you to school. You'll have plenty of time."

"O-*kay!*" I jumped out of bed and flew into my clothes. I love going out to breakfast, and Daddy takes me lots of times, but always on Saturdays, never on school days. I was dressed and ready in record time, partly because I was hurrying so, but also because I skipped my regular chores, making my bed and collecting laundry. I hate collecting laundry, and Mom is always bugging me about it. Since she wasn't there, though, she couldn't mind, and Daddy didn't seem to know that there were things I was supposed to do.

When we got to the diner, I ordered my usual Saturday morning breakfast—bacon and eggs *and* pancakes, with orange juice and hot chocolate. Neither of us had said anything about Mom yet, and I had the feeling that Daddy was avoiding it. When the waitress brought Daddy's coffee and my hot chocolate, we sipped quietly for a minute, but after a while, Daddy looked at me over the rim of his cup. "What's on your schedule today?" he asked.

"School," I answered. I meant to be funny, but Daddy answered me seriously.

"I know, honey, but what's happening at school today?"

I sighed. "Algebra quiz at nine; gymnastics practice after school. Nothing else much. Oh, yeah, soccer practice too. Five o'clock."

"How's the gymnastics going?"

I put down my hot chocolate and poked at the marshmallow, pretending I was drowning it. Why was Daddy asking me about gymnastics? It seemed weird, because that's what Mom and I always talked about. I mean, Mom helped me like a coach, and Daddy helped me with the soccer. I looked up, and Daddy was still watching me, waiting as if he really wanted to hear. "It's going pretty well," I answered.

"And algebra?"

"That's good too," I said. "Getting mostly A's."

"That's good. You're a smart girl, Sarah."

I nodded, but I looked away. Mom always told me that, and I wanted to talk about Mom now, but it was as if we had a silent agreement of some sort to talk about everything else. I drowned my marshmallow again, then looked up. "What's on your schedule today?" I asked.

"I'm going to spend the day with Mom at the hospital."

"You're not going to work?" I was surprised.

"No, not today. Mom's having some tests done, and I think she'd like it if I were there. Besides, then I'll get a chance to talk to the doctors too, and see what's going on."

I felt relieved then. We'd know by that night what was wrong, and now that Daddy had brought it up, I felt free to ask. "What's wrong with Mom? What are they testing for?"

Daddy was stirring his coffee, and he didn't look up. "Oh, I don't know exactly, Sarah. You know Dr. Kelly. He's so cautious. I think he's going to test Mom for everything he can think of."

"What's everything?"

"Here," Daddy said, looking up at the waitress who was approaching. "Here's our food." He pushed his coffee cup aside, making room for his plate, but he didn't answer my question. I kept watching him for a minute, thinking he would, but he didn't look back, and I didn't want to ask again.

I began to eat, but I kept glancing up at Daddy every so often. He looked good, handsome even, all dressed up in his suit, white shirt, and tie. Usually when we went there on Saturdays, he was in tennis clothes or old work clothes, but dressed up, he was really handsome. I looked around the diner to see if anyone was noticing us, and when I saw a woman watching me, I smiled. Then I turned back and ate my breakfast.

After we both had finished, Daddy paid the bill and drove me to school. When he dropped me off, he kissed me. "See you, honey," he said.

"See you, Daddy. Please tell Mom I love her and— you know."

Daddy smiled. "Surely will."

"Oh!" Suddenly I remembered something. "Lunch money! I don't have my lunch money."

Daddy reached into his pocket. "How much do you get?"

He didn't know how much lunch cost every day? "A dollar," I answered.

"It costs a whole dollar for lunch?"

"It's sixty-five cents, and sometimes I get an ice cream. I usually have change left," I explained quietly.

"Okay." Daddy nodded and handed me the money, then began fumbling with his key chain, trying to get a key off. "You have to get in the house this afternoon!"

"Daddy, I have a key."

"Oh. Okay." He looked at me awkwardly for a minute. "See you, honey."

"See you, Daddy." I felt awkward too, and sat there, half out of the car, just looking at him. "Bye," I said finally.

"Bye."

I slammed the car door, and as I did, I saw Daddy reach over and switch on the radio.

The rest of the day I was restless. Although the algebra test was hard, it felt good to concentrate. I could forget for a while about Mom and what was happening at the hospital. Most of the day was lousy, though, and I decided not to tell anyone except Robin that Mom was in the hospital. I'm not sure why I decided that, unless it was because I felt that if I didn't tell, no one would ask me what was wrong, and I wouldn't have to wonder myself. When I told Robin, she looked a little worried, but then she shrugged and said everything would probably be all right. Besides, she said, grownups got sick all the time.

After gymnastics practice, I went home and let myself into the house. It was silent and weird feeling. There was no sign that anybody had been there all day. Mom's usual pot of coffee wasn't on the stove. My sneakers were still on the kitchen floor, where I had left them the night before. The only sounds were the ticking of the clock, and the quiet hum of the refrigerator. I opened the refrigerator and poked around inside, then went to the bread drawer and got out some bread and put it in the toaster. But I wasn't even sure I was hungry. I looked at the clock. Ten to four. A whole hour till soccer practice. I could call Robin just to talk, but she'd think I was weird, wanting to talk when we'd just left each other five minutes before.

I went to the window. No one outside, no kids, no

joggers, not even a dog. For some reason, it reminded me of a day when I was very little and had gotten lost in a playground, but I didn't know why I remembered that just then.

I turned away from the window, suddenly fighting back tears. The toast had popped, and I took it out. Cold! I stuffed it down the disposal, reached for a tissue from a box on the counter—and then jumped about a foot because the phone rang, practically in my ear.

I grabbed it, my heart pounding. "Hello?"

"Okay!" the voice said. "How's THE KID?"

"Mom! How are you?"

"Not bad. Not great, but not bad. How was your algebra test?"

"A breeze! Bet I got an A!"

"Good girl! And gymnastics?"

"It wasn't bad. A short practice because of soccer. Robin and I worked on the ropes. I'm getting calluses on my hands."

Mom giggled. "I'm getting calluses on my rear end from sitting in this bed."

"When are you coming home?"

"I don't know yet, but I told Dr. Kelly I'm going home tomorrow, ready or not. I can't stand this place."

"Oh, Mom, are you really coming home tomorrow?"

"Well, maybe, but no promises. He may want more tests."

"What did he find? Does he know what's the matter?"

"Not yet. It takes time, Sarah. You know that. I had a bunch of tests done today, but some of them take a while

24

to get the results back. As soon as I know, believe me, you'll know, and I'll get out of here. It won't be long."

"Promise? Because I miss you." It was the first time I had said it out loud.

"I miss you too, honey. Is Daddy there?"

"Daddy? No."

"Well, he will be in a minute. He left here about fifteen minutes ago so you wouldn't be home alone."

"Oh, that's all right. I don't mind," I lied.

"Okay," Mom said. "Now I'm going to call you lots because I miss you lots. And take down my number so you can call me."

"Wait a minute." I scrambled for the chalk and went to the little blackboard that hangs on the kitchen wall and wrote down the number.

"Got to go now," Mom said. "There's somebody here to take me away for more tests, and I feel like a pincushion already. Now, Daddy will be there in a little while, okay? I'll see you in just a day or so."

"Okay, Mom. Bye." I hung up, went back to the drawer, got out more bread, and put it in the toaster. Daddy was on his way home. Mom would be home tomorrow. Suddenly I was starved.

CHAPTER
Five

🖎 MOM DIDN'T COME HOME the next day or the next. On the morning of the third day, Daddy said that if she didn't come home that day, I'd be allowed to go see her at night. But that afternoon, when I got home from school, there was a note from Daddy on the blackboard. "Sarah, please call me at the hospital as soon as you come in. You have Mom's room number. Call me there. Love you, Daddy."

I dialed the number, and that choked feeling came into my throat again, the way it always does when I'm scared or nervous.

A voice answered. It was Daddy, but he spoke so quietly, I could hardly hear him. "Hello?"

"Hello, Daddy? This is Sarah."

"Sweetheart! How are you?"

"I'm okay. How are you? How's Mom? What's happening?"

"Honey, Mom was operated on this morning. She . . ."

"Operated on!" I interrupted. "For what? Why didn't you tell me?"

"We didn't know, honey. The results of the test came in just this morning. They decided to operate immediately."

"But why? For what? What's the matter with Mom?"

For a second, Daddy didn't answer, but then he said, "It's hard to tell you about it on the phone. Besides, Mom's back from surgery now, and she's asleep. I don't want to talk too loud. As soon as she's awake, I'll leave her and come home. Okay?"

"No, you don't have to do that. She'll probably need you." I wanted him home with me, but I knew he should be with Mom too. I remembered when I had my tonsils out, how I wanted somebody with me the whole time. Mom probably wanted Daddy there.

"No, Sarah," Daddy said. "It's okay. Mom said this morning before surgery that she wanted me to go home to be with you as soon as this was over. So as soon as she's fully awake, I'll be there. Maybe we'll even go out for hamburgers or something."

"Okay, but Daddy, what was Mom operated on for?"

"Honey." He paused for just an instant, but then he said, "Honey, can I tell you about it when I get home? Can you wait till then?"

"Okay, but—but, Daddy, is she all right?"

Again that weird little pause, but then he said, "Fine. She'll be okay."

"Are you sure?"

"I'm sure. Okay, Sarah?"

"Okay," I said, but I wasn't sure it was okay at all.

I said good-bye then, my heart pounding harder than it should have been. Mom couldn't be really sick, could she? Anyway, even if she was, if they had operated they must know what was wrong, and they must have fixed it, right? I needed someone to tell me that, so without even hanging up, I put my finger on the disconnect button, then lifted it and dialed Robin's number.

She answered right away, and I told her what had happened. "So if they operated," I said, "they must know what's wrong, and they must have fixed it. Don't you think so, Robin?"

"Of course." She laughed. "They don't operate *not* to fix things, silly."

I felt a little embarrassed when she said that, as though she were making fun of me, but before I could answer, she continued. "Besides, it's probably just her appendix. I had my appendix out when I was three years old. It was yucky at first. I felt sick all the time. But then I got ice cream and ginger ale and toys, and everybody came to visit. It was neat."

"Appendix!" I said. "Of course! That's why she had that sore spot in her back and side. Why didn't I think of that?"

Robin giggled. "Because you're not a genius like me. Want to play for a while? We could skate or something."

I looked around the kitchen, where I was standing. The place was a mess. Daddy and I have always done our share of the housekeeping, but somehow it wasn't the same as when Mom was there. I knew I should really clean things up.

"Huh?" Robin was waiting for my answer. "Want to skate?"

"Okay," I said. "But I'm going to tidy up this mess in the kitchen first. I'll be ready in about fifteen minutes, okay?"

"I'll be there in five," Robin said. "If you're not done, I'll help you."

"Okay." I hung up and began buzzing around the kitchen, humming. Robin was right. I was silly to worry. I took the breakfast dishes we had left in the sink that morning and crammed them into the dishwasher. It was jam-full because we hadn't run it in days, so I put in the detergent and started it. I wiped the sink and counter tops fast and dried them off with paper towels. Then I started picking up the junk. My sneakers were still in the middle of the floor from three days earlier. Daddy had hung his jacket and tie on the doorknob the night before, and they were still there. Mom would have a fit if she could see this! I tore around the house, stuffing things into closets and cabinets. In the family room, three days of newspapers were piled on a table, and next to the TV were a plate and glass from my snack the night before. Good thing Mom hadn't seen that! I cleaned it all up, and when I finished, I stood back and admired it. It was pretty good. Whoever said housework was hard? I hadn't done a bad job at all, and it had taken only about seven minutes. Then Robin rang the doorbell, and I met her out on the steps.

We skated for about an hour, practicing circles and skating backward. We had just quit and were taking off our skates when Daddy's car pulled into the driveway. Robin picked up her skates and waved good bye. "See you tomorrow," she said to me. "Hi, Mr. Morrow!" She waved to Daddy, and he smiled at her as he got out of the car.

"Daddy!" I called, as he came up the walk. "Is Mom awake?"

Daddy nodded. He looked awfully tired and even a little messy. His tie was all sideways, and his hair was sort of rumpled, the way it gets sometimes when he's been pushing his fingers through it. "Yes," he said. He smiled at me, and it made him look a lot better. "And she said to give you big loves and big hugs. It was the last thing she said before I left. So I guess I *have* to hug you." He said it in that way we have when we're teasing each other, as if he had to hug me but didn't really want to.

I shrugged and turned away, smiling. "So don't hug me. Your hugs are gross anyway."

Daddy grabbed me from behind, and gave me a big bear hug, lifting me right off the ground. "Want to go out for hamburgers or pizza or something?"

"Oh, yeah, pizza!"

"Okay, wait till I wash up, though." He started into the house.

"Daddy?"

He stopped and turned around. "Hmm?"

"What's the matter with Mom? Why was she operated on?"

Daddy shoved his hand through his hair, and I could see why it looked like that. He made it stand practically straight up. "It's something wrong with her kidneys," he said. "She has . . . a disease. The doctors had to operate to see if they could fix it." He turned to the house again.

"Did they?"

He turned back to me. "Did they what?"

30

I sighed. Was he being deliberately dumb? "Did they fix it?"

"Well, maybe."

"Maybe! They don't know?"

"Sarah." Daddy sighed. "There's nothing simple in medicine. Things take time. They've operated. They now know what's wrong. And now they have to see how to treat it. There are medicines, things like that."

"Oh, okay." I was puzzled, but a little relieved. "So you mean that if they don't fix it with surgery, they can fix it with medicine?"

Daddy nodded. "Something like that." But I thought for a second there were tears in his eyes.

We looked away from each other, and then Daddy came to me, hugged me again, and ruffled my hair. "Let's both get cleaned up and go out for pizza, okay?" Then he held me away and smiled, and there were no tears at all, so I must have been imagining it.

"Okay," I said, and I smiled at him too, but more to make him feel better than because I really felt like it. "And wait till you see how I cleaned up the house."

He grinned at me and patted my rear end, and we both went into the house to get ready.

At the pizza place, we talked a little about Mom, but mostly we were pretty quiet. Daddy said he wasn't going back to the hospital because the doctors had given Mom some medicine for pain, so they felt it would be better if she just slept a lot.

When we got home, I went into the family room to do my homework, and Daddy went to Mom's office and closed the door. I could hear him talking for a long time on the phone, and I began to wonder if he was talking to Mom. If he was, I wanted to talk too. I went and knocked softly on the door. He didn't answer my knock, so after a minute, I opened the door quietly.

Daddy's back was to me as he sat in one of those squashy chairs, and he had the phone in his lap. Whoever he was talking to, he sounded very serious. "We just don't know yet. A lot will depend on her response to the . . ." He paused. "No, not yet. But listen, Sarah . . ."

Sarah! He was talking to Grandma, Grandma Grimes! I'm named after her, so it had to be Grandma. She lives in Florida and I miss her. I hadn't talked to her in so long! "Daddy!" I interrupted. "Is that Grandma? Can I talk to her?"

Daddy looked up, startled. "Sarah!" He put his hand over the phone. "I didn't hear you come in."

"I'm sorry. Did I scare you? But is it Grandma? Can I talk to her?"

"Yes, okay." He spoke into the phone. "It's Sarah here. She just came in. She wants to talk to you."

He handed me the phone then, and I grabbed it. Grandma and I talked about Christmas, and maybe her coming to visit, and lots of things, including the gymnastics show, but she didn't say anything about Mom, probably because Daddy had already told her all about it.

When we finished talking, we both promised to write soon, and I gave the phone back to Daddy. I went upstairs then to get ready for bed. When I had bathed and all, I climbed into bed with a book and waited for Daddy to come up and kiss me good-night. Usually Mom does that, but ever since she had been in the hospital, Daddy had been coming in to say good-night. For the longest time, I could hear him downstairs, talking quietly on the phone. I called him once, but he didn't hear me, and finally, at ten to eleven, way past my bedtime, I turned out the light. I tried to stay awake until he came in, but I must have fallen asleep, because I don't remember his kissing me good-night.

CHAPTER
Six

🖎 MOM STAYED IN THE HOSPITAL more than another whole week, and during all that time I didn't get to see her. I hardly got to talk to her, either. Daddy said it was because the medicines they were giving her—treatments, he called them—were making her too weak to have visitors. One night I heard him talking to Grandma on the phone again, and he said the treatments were making Mom sick. I didn't understand how treatments that were supposed to make you better could make you sick, and after Daddy hung up, I asked him that. He just looked at me funny, as though he were surprised to see me there, and then he got up and hugged me and said, "Let's go out for ice cream." But he didn't ever answer my question.

It was exactly one week and three days after Mom's operation that Daddy came home with the news. Next day, Mom would come home. Next day! And he said that if I wanted to, I could stay home from school.

I could barely sleep that night, and I woke up early. When Daddy left for the hospital, I stayed home to get things ready. The first thing I did was clean up the house. I vacuumed and dusted and picked up everything, until the house was as neat as when Mom was there. Then I made brownies and put them in the oven. While they were baking, I got out china and silver and set the table. I used the little room off the family room that we call the morning room. It's small and it looks over Mom's garden. In the summer, we eat there a lot because it's so sunny. I used a linen tablecloth and pink linen napkins instead of the paper napkins we usually use. Then I went out in the garden to get flowers. Mom loves flowers, and she's always cutting them and filling vases, putting them all over the house. Sometimes she puts a vase in my room too.

It was cold, and most of the flowers were already dead, but there were still chrysanthemums blooming against the wall, and some marigolds too. There were enough for the table in the morning room and for Mom's office, and then I put some in my room, just the way Mom does. There were still some left, and I put them in a vase in Mom and Daddy's room on the table next to the bed.

I went around the house then, checking. Everything was perfect. I took the brownies out of the oven, and there was nothing else to do, so I went outside to sit on the steps and wait. Right above me was the roof where Robin and I had played about two weeks before. It was weird to remember that because it seemed as though it was ages ago. Even the weather had changed so much. I remembered that we were barefoot, and Mom made us put sneakers on. Now it was cold, and most of the leaves were gone too. Just a few weeks!

A horn honked at the end of the street, and I jumped. Mom! Daddy! I flew down the steps and down the driveway. I was hopping up and down by the time Daddy pulled the car all the way up the drive and stopped. I yanked the door on Mom's side open and threw myself into her lap. I didn't know it was going to happen, but suddenly I was crying. Mom put both arms around me and rocked me back and forth, rubbing my back and running her fingers through my hair. I fought back the tears, feeling silly, and when they were mostly gone, I pulled away and looked at Mom.

She was crying too, but she didn't look at all as though she were fighting the tears, just letting them roll down her face. She took my face between her hands then and held it, looking hard at me. For some reason, her tears scared me.

"What's the matter?" I said.

"I've missed you," she answered. "I've missed you so much. And it stinks . . ." She broke off as though she were choking.

"What stinks?"

But she shook her head and didn't answer, she was crying so hard. Daddy had come around to her side of the car, and he reached in to help her out. I ducked and backed out, watching Daddy help Mom. She seemed to need his help too, and she leaned heavily on his arm. When she was standing up fully, I looked at her, surprised. She had lost so much weight that her clothes hung on her, loose, almost baggy. Her skin was funny, sort of brown, like she had a tan, but pale underneath, and there were dark rings under her eyes. But she turned to me and smiled, putting her free arm out to me. I went to her, and the three of us walked to the house together, Daddy on one side of Mom, me on the other.

Halfway up the walk, Mom stopped. "The house looks so good," she said, and she smiled.

"What?" I asked.

"The house."

I looked up myself, but shrugged. It was the same house. I guess because she hadn't seen it in so long, maybe it appeared better.

Inside the front hall, Daddy asked, "Do you want to lie down?"

"No." Mom shook her head and turned to me. "Let's sit together. We have so much to talk about, to catch up on. What smells so good?"

"Brownies. I made them for you. I set the table too. In the morning room. Come here." I took Mom's arm and pulled her gently into the morning room. With the sun shining through the window, everything was beautiful. Perfect. The china was shiny, and I remembered those silly ads on TV where the ladies look at themselves in their plates, and how Mom always laughs at that.

"Flowers!" Mom said. "Oh, Sarah, did you do this?"

I nodded, pleased. "Here!" I said, and I pulled out a chair for her. "Sit down. You too, Daddy. Do you want coffee?"

Mom seemed hesitant. "Yes, I would but . . . have you learned how to make it?"

I made a face at her. "Nah, but I can learn. It's easy, right? I'll be right back."

"Want help, Sarah?" Daddy called when I was halfway to the kitchen.

"Nope, I can do it myself." And then I added, "It's a breeze."

I heard Mom giggle, and for the first time since the car pulled in the driveway, I smiled and felt okay. That sounded like Mom.

It was harder than I thought to make coffee, and when it was finally ready and I poured it, it didn't look the way coffee is supposed to. Mom's coffee is usually dark brown, and this was sort of tan, but I guessed it would be all right. Anyway, I put it on the tray with the brownies and took everything to the morning room. Mom was sitting back in her chair, turned partway so she could see the garden. Daddy had moved his chair close and was holding her hand. Mom had a sort of quiet look on her face, but Daddy looked weird—tight and strange—and I couldn't tell what he was thinking. Then Mom turned to me and grinned. "The kid—the cook," she said.

"Wait'll you taste the coffee this kid made," I said, grinning back. I held up the glass pot for her, and the sun shining through it made it seem even paler than it was.

Mom winced, and then she laughed. "Let's try it."

I poured their coffee, and we all sat around the little table. Mom had taken a flower out of the bowl in the middle and was gently twisting it around in her fingers, but her hand was trembling. I cut a brownie for her and then one for Daddy and one for me.

"For Mom," I said, holding up the cake as though I were making a toast. "Welcome home!"

Mom held up her brownie too, and so did Daddy.

We all took bites together, but I saw Mom's mouth get all twisted suddenly, and she put a hand over it, as though she were forcing down the brownie. Her eyes filled with tears, and she put down her cake and reached out to me. She took both my hands in hers, even though I still held my brownie.

"Sarah," she said, crying, "there's just no easy way

to tell you this. It's so damn unfair. It's melanoma, a terrible kind of cancer, too advanced to do anything. It's spread to my kidneys—everywhere. They say I'm not going to get better . . .'' She broke off.

She was squashing my brownie into my hand. I pulled away.

''I'm not going to get better. . . .''

The words ran around in my head, not making any sense.

''What do you mean, 'not better'? Everybody gets better!''

''No, Sarah. Sometimes people die.''

''*No*! You're not going to die!'' Somebody was screaming, and Mom put her arms around me.

I pulled away from her and looked at Daddy. He would tell me she was lying. But he was crying too, and he was nodding.

''No, you liar!'' Somewhere in the back of my head an alarm was going off, ringing, ringing. I put my hands over my ears, but it wouldn't stop. Then, Daddy was reaching to answer the telephone. Mom had picked up the flower, the flower I had picked for her. She was rolling it between the palms of her hands, back and forth, back and forth. And some of the petals were falling on the tablecloth.

✍ I DON'T REMEMBER MUCH of the rest of that day, except that I felt hateful. Mom went to her office and closed herself in, and I went to my room and slammed the door as hard as I could. I know I was crying, and I was angry too, but why I was angry, I wasn't sure. Maybe it was because I wondered why Mom was doing this to me. Why was she sick? And what did she mean she wasn't going to get better? That wasn't fair! Besides, she couldn't know that for sure. People got better all the time. I cried for a long time, and after a while Daddy came to my room and asked if I couldn't stop. He said I was making it harder for Mom. Hard for *her*? What about me? But I didn't say that out loud, and after Daddy went, I got a sweater and left the house and ran down to the corner. It was almost three o'clock, and I would wait for Robin.

I stood there a long time, waiting and thinking, and soon kids began coming home from school. Jeff Cooper and a bunch of his friends came by, and Jeff began teasing me about playing hooky. I turned my back, trying to ignore him, but I thought about what it would be like to tell the truth, to turn around and say, "Stuff it. I wasn't playing hooky. I was home because my mom came home from the hospital. Because she's going to die." I wondered what he would say to that. But I didn't say anything at all, and the boys left. After a while, everyone was gone, but still no Robin. Then I remembered. Gymnastics practice! How could I be so dumb? I ran all the way to school and into the gym.

Robin saw me before I saw her, and she waved to me from the top of the ropes. I sat down on the crash mat and began pulling off my sneakers, getting ready to climb up, but in a second, she had slid down and was sitting beside me. "What happened? You sick today?" she asked. "How come you're here now?"

"I wasn't sick," I answered. "Mom came home from the hospital today, and my dad let me stay home to see her."

"Wow, that's great! How is she?"

"Sick."

"What do you mean, sick? She's not better?"

I shook my head. "She says she's not."

"What's the matter with her?" Robin was frowning at me. "What's wrong?"

"She has cancer, some weird kind of cancer. Her kidneys."

"Oh, God!" Robin whispered, and her eyes got wide.

I swallowed hard, then blurted it out, even though I had just promised myself that I'd never, never tell anyone. "She says she's going to die. People don't die from that—not all the time, do they?"

Robin shook her head no, but still had that awful look on her face.

"She can't die!" I said, and for the first time since

that morning, since Mom told me, it began to seem maybe real. I just looked at Robin, tears forming in my eyes, and she looked back. And then we both turned away from each other.

"Maybe they're wrong," Robin said after a while. "Doctors make mistakes, you know. And nobody can say for sure that somebody else is going to die."

I nodded miserably, but forced myself to answer. "Yeah, maybe you're right." Then I blurted out something I hadn't meant to say, something I didn't even know I was thinking. "But she's so— I mean, she's my *mother*. Mothers don't die . . ."

"They made a mistake," Robin said, and now she was beginning to sound more sure of herself. She shook her head vigorously back and forth. "Some people die, but not your mom. She's really healthy. She'll make herself get better. Not everybody dies from cancer. Lots of people live and get better. Remember Kim in fourth grade? She had bone cancer, and they moved to be nearer the hospital so she could have her treatments. And she got all better."

"But this is some weird kind of cancer, Mom said, something that starts with an *m*, but I can't remember what she called it."

"Doesn't matter." Robin sounded sure of herself. "She's going to get better."

I knew she was trying to reassure me, and I wanted to believe her. "You really think so?"

"Really." She nodded.

I didn't know how she could be so sure, but it did make me feel better. "Okay," I said. "Let's climb the ropes. But Robin . . ."

She looked at me.

"Robin, don't tell anybody, okay? I don't want anybody to know."

She nodded, and we both climbed the ropes then and worked on our routine. The gymnastics show was still many weeks away, but we had a lot of work to do. Robin hadn't said anything in a while about chinning off that bar that Mr. Anderson had warned us away from, and I didn't mention it, either, just hoping she had forgotten all about it.

When practice was over, we walked home slowly. Now that daylight-saving time was over, it was almost dark, and the darkness so early made me feel sad. "Robin?" I said. "Think you could come home with me? Maybe we could have dinner together. You could call your mom and ask?"

"Would your mom want me there—you know, being sick and all?"

"I don't think she'd mind," I answered, even though I wasn't sure of that. I was sure, though, that I didn't want to go home alone, and having Robin there would make it better. "Come on, you can call from my house."

Robin nodded and we walked the rest of the way home in silence. The porch lights were on when we got there, and lights were on in Mom's office too. I wondered what she was working on, what she was thinking about. But once inside, I could hear the stereo and smell coffee. It was the first time in weeks that things seemed normal. "Mom?" I called. "I'm home."

"In here!" The answer came from her office, and I went over and opened the door.

"Hi, Mom! I brought Robin with me, okay?"

Mom was at her desk, and she looked up and smiled at us. "Hello, Robin. It's good to see you again." She sounded happy, and she was smiling, just the way she used to, but I couldn't help noticing how tired she appeared and how the dark spots under her eyes seemed even darker in the light from the desk lamp.

"Hi, Mrs. Morrow," Robin said. "I'm glad you're home."

"Me too," Mom agreed. "Hospitals stink." She turned to me then. "I was getting worried about you. Where did you go?"

"To school. Gymnastics practice. Sorry I forgot to tell you." What I didn't tell her was that I was mad and hadn't wanted to tell her where I was going—that she could do the worrying for once. What I said out loud was, "Can Robin stay for dinner?"

Mom nodded immediately, as though she didn't even need to think about it. "I don't know what we're having, but as soon as Daddy and I decide, we'll get it started. Robin better call her mom, though."

We both nodded, and we went into the kitchen, closing the door to Mom's office behind us. In the kitchen, Robin said, "She doesn't look bad. Just tired."

I nodded. "And she's working."

"She'll be okay," Robin said. She picked up the phone and dialed her number while I stood and waited. I listened when she got her mom on the phone, but then I noticed that she had turned her back to me and was talking very quietly. I wondered if her mom was mad that she hadn't come home right away, and since I could see that she wanted some privacy, I walked away a little.

After a minute, I heard her hang up, and I turned around. "You allowed?" I asked.

Robin nodded, but she didn't say anything.

"Was she mad?" I continued.

"Nope. She just gets weird sometimes. Sad."

"Why sad?"

Robin shrugged. "I don't know, and I don't think she does, either. My father says she's depressed."

"Depressed?"

"Yeah. Sad. It's a disease—at least, that's what my father says. She takes medicine, but it doesn't always help."

"Sadness is a disease?"

Robin nodded. "I know it sounds weird, but that's what he said. But if she keeps taking her medicine, she'll get better. And she goes to a doctor, so it will help."

"I hope so." I felt uncomfortable. "Robin," I said, "I didn't know . . ."

"I know. I don't usually tell anybody. But . . ." She shrugged, but she didn't continue. Still, I thought I knew what she meant. Maybe she meant that now that I had told her about my mom, she could tell me about hers.

"I'm starved," I said, trying to change the subject. "I could eat a horse."

"Me too."

"A horse?"

We both turned. Mom and Daddy were standing in the doorway to Mom's office, their arms around each other, and they were smiling at us. "Would you settle for hamburgers?" Daddy said. "How about if we go out for some?"

"Okay!" Robin and I both said at the same time.

"Get your coats," Daddy said. "Let's go."

We got our things, and we all went down the walk together and piled into the car. Mom was leaning hard on Daddy's arm, just the way she had that morning when she came home from the hospital, but she seemed better, and she was laughing.

"Where are we going?" I asked.

"A special place," Mom answered. "I heard about it at the hospital, and I think we should try it. Horseburgers are their specialty."

"Yuck!" I answered.

I turned to Robin, and she was smiling. She poked me in the ribs, then leaned over and whispered, "Your mom is fine. She's going to be fine."

GOING OUT TO DINNER was fun, and we laughed a lot, and neither Mom nor Daddy said anything more about Mom's being sick. I kept sneaking looks at Mom, trying to see how she *really* was, but I couldn't tell much that way. Mostly, she appeared tired and kind of skinny, but not really bad.

Later that night, when I went to bed, Mom came in and sat on the side of my bed just the way she used to, and she didn't say anything about being sick then, either. But I was afraid that if she stayed, she'd start talking about it, so I yawned and told her I was super tired. I was, too. The night before, I had been so excited because Mom was coming home that I had hardly slept.

The next morning things were just the way they used to be. Mom was up early and dressed, working in her office before I even came down. I made my breakfast, and while I ate, Mom brought her coffee to the table and sat with me. Then I left for school, and Mom went back to work. While I walked to school, I thought about it. Mom looked pretty good, and she seemed just the same. So why had she said what she said yesterday? Was it just in case— *just in case*—she didn't get better? She sure looked as though she was going to be all right, just the same as always. At school, when I said that to Robin, she agreed that Mom had been just the same the night before. Exactly.

I didn't stay for gymnastics practice that day. It had been so long since I had gone home from school and found Mom there that I wanted to get home on time and see her and talk, just the way we used to. It was a little after three-thirty when I burst into the house. "Mom!" I shouted. "Hi, Mom, I'm home!"

"Hello, honey, I'm in here."

In her office, not in bed! I was so glad, because for a minute, when I opened the front door, I had been afraid I'd find her in bed like that other time.

I opened the door to her office. She was sitting in one of the big chairs, her feet up on another chair, reading from a folder in her lap. She smiled at me. "Hi, sweetheart."

"Hi. How do you feel?" I couldn't help asking it, but I turned away and looked out the window before she could answer.

"Not bad. A little tired."

"Good." I was so relieved that I smiled at her. "I'm starved. I'm going to get a snack. Want anything?"

Mom smiled back. "Not really. But you get yours, and after you're finished, there's something I want to do with you."

"Yeah, what?" Right away, I thought of clothes. We'd go clothes shopping!

"Laundry," Mom said.

"Laundry! How boring."

Mom smiled again. "How necessary."

I went back to the kitchen, feeling good but a little

puzzled. Mom had never asked me to help with the laundry before. I didn't even know how to run the washer or anything. But I guessed that if she was sick, she'd need help, at least until she was better. I made toast with cinnamon sugar and ate about half a loaf, and when I was almost finished, Mom came into the kitchen. She sat down at the table across from me.

"Looks like you haven't eaten in a week," she said.

"I'm finished now." I dusted toast crumbs from my mouth and hands and stood up. "What do you want to do about laundry?"

"I want to teach you how to do it."

"Boring," I said again.

"Necessary," Mom said again, and we both laughed.

We smiled at each other, and then Mom stood up and put both arms around me. "Oh, Sarah," she whispered.

I pulled away quickly. "Come on," I said. "Let's get it over with." I turned to the laundry room just off the kitchen. "What do I have to learn?" I reached into the dirty-clothes bin and started pulling out things, Daddy's pajamas, my jeans, my white gym socks, and all the other stuff. It smelled terrible. "Dump it in, dump in soap. How much?" I turned to Mom. She hadn't moved from where I had left her in the kitchen, but when I looked at her, she came toward me slowly.

She laughed softly and shook her head. "Honey, that's not how you do it. You have to sort wash first. Dark colors, light colors, white things."

"Oh, pooh! You sound like an ad on TV."

"Wait till your blue velour sweater comes out gray from being in with the jeans and you won't think so."

"Is that really what happens?"

She nodded, and suddenly there were tears in her eyes.

I turned away, bent over the laundry bin again, and tried to come up with things all the same color. I couldn't look at Mom, wouldn't ask her why she was crying.

Even though I didn't ask, she started to talk anyway. "Sarah, it's the nuttiest thing, but you know what haunted me in the hospital when they first told me . . . about the cancer?"

I didn't answer or look up, just stayed bent over the clothes bin.

Mom paused for a minute, then went on. "Thinking of leaving you, thinking of the little things, thinking of how you're going to have to care for yourself. And all I haven't taught you yet." She paused for a long time, then spoke again. "Stupid things, like laundry. Who's going to make sure you have your blue velour clean when you want it, or your gym suit on Monday mornings? You have to learn that, honey." I could tell she was crying, and I was crying too, but I wouldn't look up. Nobody's ever stayed head-down in a laundry bin for as long as I did.

"Here's four pairs of jeans," I said after a while, still without straightening up. "And black socks. Can they go in together?"

There was no answer, and slowly I stood up. Mom was looking at me, tears in her eyes. "You have to face it, Sarah. You have to. It won't do any good to avoid it. Please! Please?" Her eyes were pleading with me.

I just shook my head. If I didn't listen, if I made my mind as blank as possible, I could do it. I could feel nothing. I pulled the pajamas and white socks out of the washer, and put in the jeans and black socks. "How much soap?" I asked.

"A cupful," Mom answered. There was no emotion in her voice then, just sort of flat. She leaned over the washer, pushed a button. "This is for a full wash," she said. "If it's a small load, you push the one for small. Here . . ." She pushed another button marked COOL, then one that said LARGE, and then stood back. "Okay," she said. "Large for a full load. Cool water for dark things. You'll use hot water for white things."

"That's easy," I said.

Neither of us moved out of the laundry room for a while. Mom was blocking my way to the kitchen, and I'd have to look at her to get past. I was still keeping my mind blank, unfeeling. I just let it run around on things like laundry, like black socks. Mom still hadn't moved, so without looking up, I said, "Anything else?"

"Yes. Books."

I was so surprised, I couldn't help turning to her then. She nodded sadly. "Yes, books. So many books I haven't told you about, haven't read to you. I want to buy you so many books now. You won't understand some of them yet, but I want you to have them for later, for when you're older. I couldn't bear for you not to have read Isak Dinesen. She's a woman, you know. And Kazantzakis. Such funny names."

"Stop it!" Tears were running down my face, and I put my hands over my ears. "Stop it!" I almost screamed it.

"I have to!" She put her arms around me. "I have to, Sarah. There's so little time. Please?"

51

"You can't die! You can't die, can't die. You can't . . ."

I was sobbing, and Mom had her arms wrapped tight around me as she rocked me back and forth, back and forth. Tears were streaming down my face as though something had broken inside. "Can't die, can't . . ." I looked up at her then, and I almost said it. "I—I . . ." But I choked it back. "I hate you!"—that's what I was going to say. "I hate you, hate you for doing this to me. Hate you for talking about dying." But something made me stop, and Mom pulled me close. I tried to pull away, but Mom was amazingly strong, and she held me tight. And then I really couldn't stop crying. Tears just ran out until I was exhausted, till I could hardly stand up, but after a long while, I couldn't cry any more. It wasn't that I didn't want to. It was just that there were no more tears left. My breath was coming in big, shaky sobs, and Mom began patting my back softly.

After I had stopped sobbing, Mom held me away a little. "Better?" she asked quietly.

I nodded. The biggest silent lie I had ever told in my life, because I wasn't better at all. I was worse than ever. Because now that I had begun to cry, now that I had begun to let it in, I was beginning to believe it was true.

CHAPTER
Nine

 AFTER THAT, we went clothes shopping and then to the bookstore. Neither of us said any more about what we had just talked about, but it was different from the day before—for me, anyway. I didn't have the feeling that I had to keep running away from Mom to keep her from saying anything.

At the clothes store, I got new jeans and a new winter jacket because my old one had gotten so small that my wrists stuck out. And then I got a new velour sweater, a pink one, and after that we went to the bookstore. I picked out a lot of books from the young-adult section, and Mom picked out about a dozen books from the grown-up shelves. I didn't even want to look at them, but I didn't say that to Mom. She asked me to put them in my bookcase so someday I'd have them when I wanted them. I knew I would never read them, though, and secretly I gave them a name—getting-ready-to-die books. I would never read getting-ready-to-die books, ever. So when I got home, I hid them in the back of my bookcase, and then I began reading the books I had picked out.

Dinner was normal enough, and afterwards I went up to take my bath. I soaped myself all over and slid under the water, as though I could wash away everything that had happened that day. Usually I take a book into the bathroom with me to read in the tub, but I had forgotten to bring the one I had started that day. I looked around, then reached out to the little stand that has some of my other books in it. I found an old one and picked it up. It's called *Summer of the Swallows*. It's all about a kid named Ellie who gets stung by a bee and dies. I used to like to read it because it's a sad book, and sometimes it's fun to feel sad—about a book. I would sit in the bathtub and cry because Ellie had died, and then I would go to my room, and the light would be on and Mom would come and kiss me good-night, and it felt good.

I started the book again. I've read it so many times, I have it memorized, practically. The words just slid across my brain, blanking everything else out. I was with Ellie and the swallows . . .

There was a knock on the bathroom door. "You okay, honey?" It was Mom.

"Uh-huh."

"You're taking forever."

"I'm reading."

"It's way past your bedtime."

"That's okay."

"Want me to make you something to eat? A little snack?"

"No thanks." I felt full, as though even the thought of food would make me throw up. I looked down at my stomach. It was shiny from the soap and water, and it was flat, nice and flat. Still, Robin and I always want to lose at least another pound, and we're always talking about going on a diet, but we never do. I wouldn't have a snack, and I could tell Robin that I had already started my diet. She'd be jealous.

There was silence at the bathroom door, but I could tell that Mom was still there. "You're sure you're okay?" she called after a minute.

"Mom, I'm sure! I'm too old to drown in the bathtub."

I heard her giggle, and I knew then that she would leave me alone. I read some more until I had finished the whole book. It was a short book, and I'm a fast reader, and there were even parts I could skip, I knew them so well. For some reason, this time, I didn't cry at all about any of the things that used to make me sad. The only part that seemed sad was the part where they go to the cemetery and see the hole that was dug for the casket. A hole for Ellie. A hole for Mom. I finished the book, then got out of the tub and dried off.

In my room, I got into my pajamas and into bed, then turned off the light and waited for Mom to come kiss me good-night. I didn't want to talk. I didn't want anything but for this day to be over. I wanted to go to sleep. In a minute I saw the door open, and the light from the hall slipped in. "Sarah? You awake?"

"Hmm," I muttered.

"You didn't even say good-night." I turned over and closed my eyes, but I could tell that Mom was crossing to the bed.

"I'm too tired," I murmured sleepily.

"But I feel bad when you don't say good-night."

I wanted to tell her to stop it when she said that. I didn't want to know that I made her feel bad. "I'm sorry,"

I whispered, and for about the millionth time that day, I felt ready for another cry, but I fought it back. "Just tired." I held up my face for a kiss, then turned over to the pillow.

Mom patted and rubbed my back a little. "I understand," she said, but I wondered if she did. I didn't understand it myself.

I heard the mattress sigh as Mom got up off the bed, then heard her go to the door. I opened my eyes, saw the door close, the light from the hall disappear—and then, for some reason, I couldn't stay in bed. I felt as though if I stayed there, everything would catch up with me, as if things were waiting out there for me. I got out of bed, walked over to the window, and looked out at the night. I wondered if I could see Robin's window from here, but of course I couldn't. Four blocks is a long way, and even if I could see a light, I wouldn't know which one was hers.

A door closed below me, and I looked down. Two figures were outside, standing in the dark, their faces turned up to the sky. Mom and Daddy. Daddy's arm was around Mom's shoulder, and they both stood, heads turned up. Daddy—how was he feeling? He had looked so awful for weeks, and I now knew why. He had probably been crying. I looked down at the yard again, but they were gone, maybe taking a walk around the block.

I crept back into bed. Alone, I would be all alone. And Daddy would be all alone, too. Both of us. No! I sat up and switched on the light. I had cried enough. I wouldn't cry any more.

I got out of bed again and went to my bookcase, reached to the top, and got down my hamster's cage. Flicker, my hamster. I took him out and let him run around on my hand for a while. He's soft and funny, his nose squiggling and twisting as he tries to smell me. Sometimes, if I put one finger in front of his face, he bites, but he doesn't do it to be mean. He just bites whatever is around. If I put my whole hand out, though—not just a fingertip—he doesn't bite. I lay on the floor and let him run up and down my arms, all over my stomach, and even on my face. When he crawled to the floor, I scooped him up and set him back on my stomach again. The house was so still. I wished Mom and Daddy would come back from their walk.

I fed Flicker some hamster food and some hamster treats, and he took them all and stuffed them in his cheeks. I laughed out loud and wished Robin were there, or Mom, so I could show them. His cheeks got round like a chipmunk's, and then he headed back for his cage. He always spits out the treats in a corner of his cage and saves them for later. It looks like his food cabinet or refrigerator in there. When he got back inside, I closed the cage tightly, then put a book over it, because sometimes he bumps against it so hard he knocks the top off. I opened my bedroom door then, and listened to hear whether Mom and Daddy were downstairs yet. Why hadn't I talked to Mom when she came to say good-night? Why had I pretended to be sleepy? It was so quiet now.

Still no sound down there. I was shivering suddenly, but I couldn't bear the thought of going back to bed—not yet, not until they were back from their walk. I went to my closet for my robe, but then I realized I didn't want my own robe. I wanted Mom's, the one we tease her about and call her woolly lamb robe. It's white and fuzzy and practically worn out, and half the buttons are missing, but

57

Mom wears it when she's especially cold or when she feels down. She says it makes her feel better. I went to her room, tiptoeing in case they had come back, because I didn't want to have to explain.

I found the robe, wrapped myself in it, then went back to my room. I turned out the light and looked out the window again. It was a cold, clear night, the stars shining brightly. When you are dead, what do you do? Are you really in heaven? Is there such a place? Are there angels and stars, and do you hang around in the stars? Or when you're dead, are you just plain dead? Stupid questions! Stupid little-kid questions!

I began to cry again, tears running down my face. I stood at the window, wrapped in Mom's robe, and it was warm, but it didn't help. I must have been crying so hard that I didn't notice the light slide across the floor again as someone opened the door a crack. Then Daddy was beside me. He lifted me up as easily as though I were a little baby and carried me across the room to my bed, and he sat me in his lap. I didn't know that it would feel almost as good as Mom's. Then we both cried for a long time.

CHAPTER
Ten

It was funny how the days went after that. I guess you can't keep on crying forever, because things began to seem awfully normal. Thanksgiving came and went, and Grandma and Grandpa Grimes came from Florida to visit, and then Christmas was coming. The gymnastics show was coming too, and there was a lot to get ready for. Mom didn't say much any more about being sick, and she didn't say anything at all about dying, and I didn't think about it a lot—at least, not in the front of my mind. But in the back, it was always there, like those tapes they play in the dentist's office, that weird, dreary sound in the background that you can't shut out. Mostly though, Mom looked better, and things seemed pretty much the way they used to be.

It was on one of those normal days that I came home from school and found Mom up on a ladder in the morning room. The furniture was covered with big cloths, the rug was turned back, and all the pictures were off the walls. Mom had a can of spackle in her hand and a putty knife. She was filling the nail holes in the wall and grinned at me as I came in. "I can't stand this room. What color are we going to paint it?"

"Huh? Paint?"

"Yes. Choose a color." She pointed to a chart that was half buried in a chair, underneath some figurines that were piled there.

"Mom, you're nuts! This room is fine. And, anyway, how can you get it done in time?"

"What do you mean, in time?" She paused and looked at me, the putty knife held in midair, and there was a stillness not only in her hands, but in her face.

"Before Christmas! Christmas is only two weeks away."

"Oh." Mom turned back to the wall then, and I couldn't see the expression on her face any more. "No problem. You know me. I can finish a room in two days flat." She laughed then. "*With* a little help."

"Un-uh! Not me! I hate painting, and you know it."

"Aw, come on, Sarah. Please?" She sounded like a little kid.

"No way! Besides, I have gymnastics practice every day after school."

"You could help when you come home."

"*Mom!*" I hate it when she does that to me, makes me feel guilty.

"Okay," she said. "But you have to help me pick out a color."

I uncovered one of the chairs, scooped some magazines out of the seat, and sat down with the chart. "It has to be bright," I said.

"For sure."

"Blue? Light blue?"

"I've thought about that. Maybe."

"Or . . ." I flipped through the chart. "Here's a good one. How about this?" I held it out. It was pink, almost a peachy color.

Mom made a face, and I went back to the chart. "How about a yellow or gold? Look." I held the booklet up for her to see. There was a page with the bands of color from bright yellow to dark, mustardy golds. The dark ones were yucky.

"Mmm," Mom said. "Some of them are nice and springy looking. When spring comes and the flowers are in bloom again, this room would be nice, almost like the outdoors—sun color."

"Yeah, that'd be nice. Mom, where are we going to put the Christmas tree this year?" I knew I was changing the subject, but I had gotten used to listening to a sound in the back of my head, a warning bell that went off, and when Mom started talking about spring, the alarm sounded. "Huh? Where will we put it this year?"

"Where would you like it?"

"In here maybe, if it's finished in time?" We've never had the tree in the morning room, even though it's been practically everywhere else in the house. Sometimes it's in the living room, and sometimes in the family room. Once, when I was very small, it was in the front hall. That was because I had wanted to see it, first thing when I came down in the morning.

"That would be nice," Mom said. "With all these windows, people could see the lights from outside." She paused, and even though she was facing the wall, when she spoke again, I could tell that she was smiling. "Of course," she said slowly, "I'd probably have to have some help with the painting. I mean, I don't see how I could paint *and* do the Christmas decorating . . ."

"Oh, all right! Honestly, Mom, you're a pain! Painting this room was your idea."

"Tell you what. How about if you take off from school to do it with me?"

"Really?" I squealed and jumped out of the chair, spilling magazines all over the place.

"Why not? You're a good student, so you wouldn't miss much."

"What would I tell my teachers?"

"Why would we have to tell them anything but the truth?"

"That I took two days off to paint with my mother? I couldn't do that. It would be an unexcused absence, and I'd get F's for the entire two days' work."

"Unexcused absence?" Mom had a puzzled look on her face.

"Yeah, the only way you get an excused absence is if you're sick or have a doctor's appointment, or sometimes if you're on a trip with your parents, although even that's a hassle. You practically have to prove that your parents couldn't take the trip any other time. You know that. It's no problem, though. I'll just tell them I'm sick."

Mom turned back to the wall, and she didn't say anything more, just worked with the putty knife for so long that she must have made the smoothest spot in the whole house.

"Something wrong?" I said finally.

"Not really."

"I don't believe you." I paused. "Is it because I said I'd lie?"

Mom took a deep breath, then let it out slowly. When she spoke, it sounded as though she were measuring every word. "I love you, Sarah, and I want to be with you as much as possible. I want to spend the time with you painting this room, and I'll even lie if I have to in order to get that time. That's not what's bothering me. But something else is bothering me, scaring me, even. You see, I've been feeling so frantic about time, about not having enough time, but lately, the past few days, I'm thinking I might have a lot of time. Plenty of time."

I looked at her, puzzled, not sure what she meant.

"Sarah, I think I might beat this. I think I might get better."

Right then, I wanted her to stop. She had said the one thing I had wanted so much to hear, and if she kept on talking, she might take it back.

"I know you're going to get better. Robin knows it too. We've always known." I was lying, but it wasn't a complete lie, and it didn't matter, anyway. "Come on, what color are we"—I paused and smiled at her—"*we* going to paint this room?"

"Yellow. Sun color," she said, laughing, but there were tears in her eyes at the same time. "Sun yellow." She began laughing harder, and I looked at her quickly because there was something odd about her laugh, almost hysterical. After a minute, though, she took a deep, trembly breath, wiped her eyes, and stopped laughing. "They don't think so, you know. The doctors don't think so, but every time I go in for a test, they're amazed how well I'm doing. I went in today, and they couldn't believe how well I was."

"I told you. I know!" I said. "I know you're going to be all right. And we're going to paint this room sun color. For Christmas. And for spring."

Mom laughed then, but it was a regular laugh, not like that nervous one of before. "Wait till Daddy comes home and sees this mess."

I laughed too, because Daddy was always having a fit when Mom suddenly took it into her head to do things around the house, like the time she moved every single piece of furniture in every room. "Should we tell him he has to help too?" I asked.

"No way," Mom said. "He's a bear about things like that. That's why I do it myself. But I'll tell you what." She looked at her watch. "He'll be home in a minute. How about if we ask him to take us to the paint store?"

I laughed again. "Okay, we'll meet him in the driveway and tell him we're hitching a ride."

"Get your coat," Mom said.

I got mine, and she took hers from the closet, then stopped in front of the mirror in the front hall, wiping smudges of spackle and paint chips from her face and hair. "I look a wreck," she said.

"You look great." I smiled at her, and she grinned back and put an arm around my shoulder.

The two of us went down the driveway to the street. "Should we go to the paint store?" Mom said. "Or should we take off for California?"

"California, for sure," I answered. "But the paint store first."

We sat down on the curb then, pretending we really were hitch-hikers, talking about things the way we always used to talk, about maybe really taking a trip to California the next summer. And when Daddy drove up, we were still sitting there, and like real hitch-hikers, we stuck out our thumbs.

DADDY TOOK US to the paint store, although he thought we were weird for sitting on the curb in the dark. Later we all went to McDonald's for dinner. While we were there, we made a plan: Mom and I would paint the morning room together; Daddy would put up the outside lights and set up the tree. On Saturday, the Saturday before Christmas, we would have a party. It would be a grownups' party and kids' party, too, and each of us would invite some friends. There weren't many people I wanted to invite, just Robin and maybe Julia from gymnastics. But Mom and Daddy planned to invite lots of people, their best friends—the Arnolds and the Hardings and the Steiners—and lots of others, including Daddy's partner, Mr. Alden, and his wife. That didn't make me happy because Mr. Alden is a fake, has that phony, super-friendly way of talking, but I guessed I wouldn't have to talk to him much, anyway.

The next week flew by. I took the days off to paint with Mom, and we worked from morning till dark. It was fun. Finally, it was Saturday, the morning of the party, and I woke early to the smell of coffee and pancakes. I sat up, reached out to my bedside table, got a book, and took it to bed with me. A Saturday morning with a good book in bed, my parents downstairs, and the house warm and nice made me happier than anything else in the world. I lay back to enjoy it, but it lasted only a minute. I was just too excited to stay in bed, so I got up, put on my robe, and went downstairs.

In the kitchen, Daddy was at the stove, wearing that big blue apron he wears when he cooks. He smiled at me as I came in. "Hey, Punkin, you're up early for a Saturday."

"Too excited to sleep. Besides, it smells so good."

" 'Cause I'm an A-number-one cook."

"Yup. Where's Mom?"

"Still sleeping. She was tired. All that painting you two have been doing was hard work."

"Yeah, but doesn't the room look pretty?"

"I love it." Daddy grinned at me. "Especially since I didn't have to paint it."

I sat down at the kitchen counter. Daddy poured a big glass of orange juice for me, filled it with ice the way I like it, and handed it to me. He started to turn back to the stove, then stopped, came back and sat beside me, his arms folded on the counter. He turned toward the window with a faraway look in his eyes "You know what, Sarah?"

"What?"

"I think I'm about as happy today as I've ever been in my life."

He looked happy too, and I smiled at him. "Yeah," I said. "I know it's going to be a good party. Lots of food, and lots of—"

"Friends," Daddy interrupted, as though he knew what I was going to say. "Good food and good friends and a wonderful party, a Christmas party." Although he still wasn't looking at me, I was suddenly startled, because I thought there were tears in the corners of his eyes.

"Daddy?"

"What?" But he didn't turn to me.

"Uh, why don't we take Mom breakfast in bed?"

"Oh, good idea!" Daddy stood up and looked right at me, and if there were tears before, they were gone now. "You get a tray ready, and I'll finish the pancakes."

Together, we made a big tray of food for Mom and some pancakes for Daddy and me, too, so Mom wouldn't have to eat upstairs all by herself. While Daddy did the pancakes, I went to the morning room and cut a little twig from the Christmas tree, hung a tiny, shiny Christmas ball on it, and put it in a vase on the tray. I used cloth napkins too, green ones for Christmas, and when we had it all ready, we went upstairs, me carrying the tray, Daddy carrying the coffee and hot pancakes.

We tiptoed into Mom's room and put the tray and coffee pot on her bedside table. "Good morning!" I said. "Wake up. Room service!"

Dad went to the windows and pulled up the blinds, letting in the cold, winter light. With the room suddenly bright like that, I could see Mom lying on her back in the bed, unmoving. "Mom? Mom!"

I must have sounded frightened because in an instant Daddy was at my side. Both of us were looking at Mom. I looked up at Daddy then, fear making my throat tight, but he was just smiling down at Mom. "She sure can sleep," he said softly.

"How do you know she's asleep?"—I wanted to say

it, but didn't. I looked back at Mom. "The way you can tell she's sleeping," I told myself, "is that the blankets are moving up and down, nice and regular, up and down, just the way they're supposed to. Dummy." I swallowed hard, letting the fear ease away, feeling stupid for being scared. Sitting down on the bed then, I shook Mom's arm, but I kept my face turned away from Daddy so he wouldn't know how stupid I'd been and what dumb things I'd been thinking.

When I took Mom's arm, her eyes opened and instantly she smiled at me. "Well." She took a deep breath, and wrapped an arm around my waist. "What's the meaning of waking me up so early?" she said.

"The meaning is breakfast," I announced. I stood up, picked up the tray then, and held it out in front of her.

"Ooh!" Mom smiled and struggled to a sitting position. "Am I hungry!"

"Me too."

It took a few minutes to serve the pancakes and pour the syrup, but eventually we were ready. Daddy took his plate and sat in the chair beside the bed, and I took mine and sat cross-legged on the foot of the bed. Mom had the tray set up in front of her, all to herself. We ate quietly for a while, and I was surprised at how hungry I was. Mom must have been hungry too, because she ate practically everything on her plate. After a while, she looked up at Daddy and me. "Know what?" she said.

"What?"

"I think this is the happiest day of my whole life."

I laughed and looked at Daddy, expecting him to tell

Mom what he had just told me downstairs, but he was only smiling at Mom, so I didn't say anything, either, but I thought, "Me too."

The rest of the day was a madhouse. The phone rang constantly, and the caterer brought the food and chairs. A florist came with the flowers for the hall table and a centerpiece for the dining room table. Mom, Daddy, and I made hors d'oeuvres and set out plates and silverware, and Daddy laid a fire in the fireplace. It had begun to snow a little, and I was both excited and scared—excited because it was the first snowfall of the year, and scared because if it snowed too hard, people couldn't come.

I thought of Grandpa and Grandma then. Grandpa especially loved the snow. I wished so much they could be here, but they had both come down with the flu. Grandpa had written and told me to save him a snowball if it snowed. I knew he was fooling, but I ran outside anyway, made him a snowball and came back and put it in the freezer.

I ran back and forth to the window all day, checking, but although the sky was gray and heavy, the snow just fell lightly. By six o'clock, when we went upstairs to get dressed, there was only about an inch covering the grass and trees, piling up in little crests on the railing out front.

I didn't have to think about what I was going to wear. Robin and Julia and I had already planned it—our best jeans and pretty shirts. I was going to wear my favorite blue velour. But when I went up to my room, on my bed was a dress: a long red dress with lace at the neck and sleeves and a green velvet ribbon around the waist. It was made of something soft, maybe silk, and when I held it up to me, it came all the way down to the floor. "Mom!"

I shouted, and I ran down the hall to her room. "Mom, is this mine? Did you buy this for me?"

Mom was smiling happily. "Uh-huh."

"Oh, it's so beautiful! I love it." I did too, but I didn't know whether I should wear it that night, because Robin and Julia probably didn't have anything even nearly like it.

"It's all right if you don't want to wear it tonight," Mom said, as if she were reading my mind. "I just wanted you to have it. It's so pretty."

"Oh, Mom!" I went to her, hugged her gently, then held the dress up in front of me and danced around. "I want to wear it, but I'm not sure. Oh, what should I do?"

Mom just smiled.

"Robin and Julia will feel dumb if they come in jeans and I'm all dressed up. And it's awfully late to call and ask them to wear something else."

"Then maybe you'd better not wear it. Save it for Christmas."

"But I *want* to wear it."

"I know." Mom laughed. "Such problems." She turned to the mirror and began putting on her make-up. I knew she wouldn't give me any more help, so I turned to go back to my room. But for just a second, I watched her in the mirror. She looked good, but something was funny about her skin, or maybe it was her make-up, because she looked sort of tan. Well, maybe not tan, but yellowish, the way you get at the end of summer when your tan is fading. She saw me watching her in the mirror and smiled at me. I smiled back, then went back to my room. I debated for just another second about calling Robin and Julia, but decided that wouldn't be fair. I laid the dress on the bed, spread out the way Mom had it before. I couldn't wait till they came so I could show it to them.

It seemed like forever until the first guest arrived, and when the doorbell rang, I ran to answer it. It was the Arnolds, and they were carrying some wrapped packages. They came in, and hugged me, and gave me a package. Presents? I didn't know I was going to get a present! Before I could open it, the bell rang again, and the Steiners came in and then the Hardings, all of them stamping snow from their feet. I was busy taking coats and saying hello to everybody. Then Robin and Julia arrived together, and they both looked so pretty in their soft sweaters that I was happy that I hadn't asked them to change.

It was definitely the best party we ever had, and probably the best party I've ever been to. There was lots to eat and drink and lots of music and noise, and even the grownups were fun to be with. Then late, right before we were to have dinner, someone suggested that we go out Christmas caroling. Everybody agreed it would be fun, so we got out coats and boots and scarfs. Someone got a song book from the piano, and we all went outside. It was snowing harder, and we went to the end of the street, stopping in the cul-de-sac that faces a group of houses. Mr. Alden began singing. "Oh, holy night . . ." his voice rang out. For the first time since I've known him, he didn't sound at all fake or super-friendly, just real, and he had a beautiful voice.

The rest of us joined in. "The stars are brightly shining. It is the night of the dear . . ."

I looked at Mom and Daddy. Mom was shivering a

little, the way she always did in the cold, and Daddy had his arm wrapped around her shoulder. They saw me looking at them, and they smiled. Mom made a motion to me to join them, but I just stood watching them, remembering what Daddy had said that morning, remembering what Mom had said and how I had echoed it in my mind. I wondered if they were thinking it too—"This must be the happiest day of my life."

CHAPTER
Twelve

🖎 SUNDAY WAS A long, quiet day. The snow had stopped during the night, and in the morning a pale sun came out, making a white ring in the heavy sky. There were about eight inches of snow on the ground, and although I thought it would be fun to go out in it, I was tired after being up until two o'clock the night before. Mom was tired too and thought she might be coming down with a cold or flu, because her arms and legs were hurting a lot. Most of the day she stayed in bed, and Daddy sat in a chair beside her, reading the Sunday papers, while I lay on the floor between them looking at the comics. For a while, it was very comfortable and quiet.

We talked about the party, about how everybody looked and who made the funniest jokes, and about how good the food was. Mom and Daddy talked about who said what to whom. Around three o'clock, Mom said she wanted to take a nap, and I was getting bored. I put on my heavy clothes, and went out in the snow for a while.

When I came in, Daddy made dinner—mostly leftovers from the party—and Mom came downstairs to eat, still wearing her robe. She said her legs were still hurting, and I thought again how yellow she looked, but I didn't say anything. Then, right after dinner, we went upstairs to our rooms and to bed.

Next morning, I got up quickly, dressed, breakfasted, and said good-bye to Daddy even before Mom was up. I was anxious to get to school early because that was the day of the gymnastics show and the last day before school closed for the Christmas holidays. The teachers excused kids who were in the show from all classes so we could have one final rehearsal. Robin and I went through our routine again. We had worked really hard, and we knew we had the best routine in the show. It had two parts, the floor routine and the ropes. On the floor, we did rolls, cartwheels, backward walkovers, and one midair flip each while we spotted each other in case one of us fell. On the ropes, we raced up and down, switching ropes halfway up. In one part, we dangled by our legs.

There was only one thing that worried me: Robin hadn't said anything in a long time about chinning off the cross bar, yet I knew her well enough to know she hadn't forgotten about it. I was afraid to ask, though, because if by some chance she *had* forgotten, mentioning it would remind her. I just prayed that she had decided not to do it, because if she did it in the show, she'd be in real trouble.

On the way home, we discussed again what we would wear that night, because we wanted to dress exactly alike. We decided to wear white shorts, our white Adidas shirts with red trim, and short white socks with red balls on them. We parted at the corner and agreed to meet at the gym at six-thirty, long before anyone else, so we could have one last practice.

When I got home and opened the door, the odor of the

75

Christmas tree greeted me and I breathed in deeply. Christmas everywhere. "I'm home, Mom!" I shouted.

There was no answer. I listened for the typewriter from her office, but it was silent.

"Mom?" I opened the door. "Mom?"

No Mom, not at her desk anyway. I raced up the stairs. "Please don't be in bed," I prayed. "Mom?" I went in the bedroom, but she wasn't there, and the bed was made, smooth and neat.

I ran downstairs, my heart beginning to pound hard, and into the kitchen to look at the blackboard. Maybe she had gone shopping and had left me a note that I hadn't seen. There was no note on the blackboard. "Mom!" I shouted again, and suddenly I was angry. "Mom!" Where was she? Why was she scaring me like this? "*MOM!*" I screamed at the top of my lungs.

I went to the garage, checking. Her car was still there, so maybe she had just gone for a walk in the snow or to visit a neighbor. But I knew she'd never do that on a workday.

Back inside, I stood in the kitchen, listening silently, as though if I were very quiet, I could hear where she was. The only sounds were the clock on the wall, ticking loudly, and the smooth hum of the refrigerator. It all reminded me of the first day Mom had gone to the hospital, and I knew suddenly that that was where she was now. I don't know how I knew, but I knew.

I picked up the phone and dialed Daddy's number at work. His secretary, Mrs. Corrigan, answered, and I used the most grown-up voice I had. "Is Mr. Morrow there?" I asked.

There was just the tiniest pause. "Is this Sarah?" she asked.

"Yes, it is."

"Oh." Another pause, and then she said, "No, your Daddy isn't here right now. Uh, where are you?"

"Home."

"Oh, can you wait a minute?"

"Okay."

She went away from the phone, and I could hear quiet talk in the background. In a few seconds Mr. Alden came on the phone. "Well, hello, Sarah!" he said, and his old hearty-fake voice was back.

"Hello, Mr. Alden. Is my father there?"

"No, he's not. Sarah, are you at home?"

"Yes!" I was annoyed. I had already told Mrs. Corrigan that, and besides, I didn't see what business it was of theirs, anyway.

"Uh, why don't I come over there for a while? Your dad is, uh, with your mother, uh. They didn't leave you a note?"

"Mr. Alden, what do you mean?" I asked. "If my father's with my mother, where are they?"

Another pause, but then he said, "I'm, uh, not sure, but your mom wasn't feeling too great. I . . . think your dad took her to the doctor's."

He was lying. I could tell by his voice he was lying, that he knew they had gone to the hospital and that he probably knew I knew.

"Is she in the same hospital she was in before?" I said as calmly as I could manage, even though I felt as though I were going to cry.

"I'm not sure. Listen, Sarah, I'm coming over there right now. I'll be with you in a few minutes."

"No, I'm not going to be here," I lied. "I have a gymnastics show tonight, and I'm going over to my friend's house to practice. I'll just leave them a note."

"Are you sure that's all right?" he asked, but I thought I heard relief in his voice.

"I'm sure. I'm on my way right now."

"Would you give me the number at your friend's house?" Mr. Alden asked. "In case your dad calls, or . . . in case . . ." He didn't seem to know why he wanted Robin's number. I didn't know why, but I didn't want to give it to him, either. Therefore, I did something I'd never done before, and I did it as calmly as I had when I asked about the hospital. I gave him the wrong number. I used Robin's number but twisted the last two digits from 0-9 to 9-0. Then I said good-bye and hung up.

I sat down at the table, staring out the window, choking back tears. They had to be at the hospital, and it must have been an emergency because they'd never leave without writing me a note. Even the few times Mom had forgotten to leave me a note, she returned within a minute or two of the time I got in the house. And that night was the night of the gymnastics show, a show I had worked on for three whole months. Nobody would be there to see me. Thinking that, thinking about the show and the other kids, I felt almost ashamed—embarrassed, sort of—that I'd be the only kid in the show who wouldn't have parents there to watch. Then it came to me that I didn't care whether they came or not. I didn't even care if Mom was sick. But I decided not to tell anybody, not even Robin. I would just pretend they were out there somewhere. There'd be so many faces in the gym, that no one could tell who was there anyway.

The phone began ringing then, and I reached out to answer it, but then I realized that it might be Mr. Alden, checking to see whether or not I was really at Robin's. Because I didn't want him to come over, I let it ring for a long, long time.

CHAPTER
Thirteen

🖋 FOR ABOUT AN HOUR, I stayed in the house alone. The phone rang about a jillion times, but I ignored it. I figured Mr. Alden had already called the wrong number I had given him and was trying to call me to get the right one. I realized, too, that it might be Mom or Daddy calling to tell me where they were. For some reason, I didn't want to talk to them, didn't want to find out what was happening. Also, I knew that even if Mom was back in the hospital, sooner or later Daddy would come home to me.

After about an hour, when it was beginning to get dark and still no one was there, I had to get out, away from the house completely. I put on my white shorts and shirt and the socks with the red balls on them, put my sweatsuit on top, then my ski jacket. It was still hours till the show, but I left for school, anyway. If the gym was open, I could practice till Robin got there, and that way I wouldn't have to wait around the house.

It was cold as I walked back to school, and I had forgotten my gloves. I thought of going back for them, but instead stuffed my hands in the pockets of my jacket. Thoughts were spilling around in my head. Mom was sick, really sick, and maybe this was bad, worse than last time.

No, remember she said just a few weeks ago that she thought she was going to beat this. She said so! She even said the doctors were surprised at how well she was doing. Then I thought about the gymnastics show. All that work, and she wasn't even going to be there to see it. If she really cared, she'd be there. Even though part of me knew that was ridiculous, that she couldn't help it if she was sick, part of me was mad at her too. And I couldn't help that either.

At school, I went around to the gym door. The lights were on inside, and I looked through the frosted glass, but I couldn't see any figures moving around. I pulled at the door, but it didn't budge. Then I tried the other one, but that didn't open either. Should I knock? If Mr. Anderson was there, wouldn't he want to know why I had arrived so early? I couldn't wait outside in the cold, though, so I knocked good and hard, but no one came.

I tugged at the doors again. The handle was metal and so cold that it felt as though my fingers would stick to it, the way wet fingers stick to ice-cube trays. I stuck my hand back in my pocket. What should I do? I could walk to Robin's house very slowly, trying to use up as much time as possible. Then the two of us could walk to school together.

I turned and started back to Robin's house. I counted steps, forcing myself to go slowly. One step, think of something, a line of a song—yeah, one line with each step. "Raindrops on roses and whiskers on kittens." I recited the song as slowly as I could, the whole thing, one step at a time. But I was freezing, poking along like that, and when I looked at my watch, it was only five-fifteen.

I tried something different. The wind was blowing right in my face, but if I walked backward, it would be warmer—and it would take longer, too. I turned around and tried it. Again, one step for each line of the song. I chose another of my favorites. "The sun will come out tomorrow . . ."

It was taking too long, and I was shivering. And then I did it. Took another backward step and crashed right into a telephone pole. I rubbed my head and felt tears rushing to my eyes. I turned and began to run. I didn't care if I did get there too early. I ran all the rest of the way to Robin's house.

It was dark going up the walk, but I could see lights on at the back of the house. I rang the doorbell, and in a minute Robin opened the door. "Hey!" she said. "Where've you been? I've been calling you and calling you!"

"Oh, I, uh, took a walk. Went to school to see if the gym was open yet. But it's not."

"You want to come in?" Robin held the door wide, but she looked embarrassed.

I tried to pretend I didn't notice her embarrassment. I knew—I've known Robin for so long—I knew nobody went to her house. Whatever was wrong with her mother made it too hard for her to have anybody come visit. But I was too cold to stay outside any longer, so I said, "Yeah, okay."

"Who is it, Robin?" A voice called from the back of the house where the kitchen was.

"It's . . . Sarah."

There was a long pause while Robin and I looked at one another, and I began to wish I hadn't gone there. I started to say I would leave, but Robin put one hand to her mouth, as though asking me to be quiet.

"Well, ask her in," Mrs. Harris said finally. "And for heaven's sake, shut the door."

"Yes, Mom." Robin took a deep breath and smiled at me. "It's okay," she whispered. "Come on in."

She led me down the hall and into the kitchen, where the light was on. Mrs. Harris was at the stove, her back to me, and she didn't turn around when I first came in. I felt so awkward. Should I say hello?

Robin took care of that by speaking first. "Mom, you know Sarah?"

Slowly Mrs. Harris turned around. At first, all I noticed was how much she resembled Robin or how Robin resembled her—those same great big, wide eyes. But the next thing I noticed was that she seemed terrified, and from the way she was looking at me, it seemed as though I was the one she was afraid of. I felt as though I should turn away from her, to make her stop being scared, so I stared down at the floor and said, "Hello, Mrs. Harris."

"Hello, Sarah," she said. Her voice was sweet and didn't sound as scared as she looked. "You must be frozen," she said after a minute.

I nodded, still afraid to look at her.

"Would you like . . . some hot chocolate?"

"Oh, no," I said. "That's okay."

"Why not?" she asked.

It seemed such a funny question, I couldn't help looking up at her, surprised. "I . . . I don't know. I mean, I just don't want you to go to any trouble."

She didn't answer, but she turned back to the stove and reached to a cabinet above and got some cocoa.

"Mom, I'm going to get dressed for the show, okay?" Robin asked.

Still without turning around, Mrs. Harris nodded. "And when you're ready, I'll have some hot chocolate ready."

"Thanks, Mom." Robin went to her mom and kissed her. Something about the way she hugged her mom close made me think that Robin was the mother and her mom was the child. Robin even smoothed her mother's hair away from her face a little, the way Mom does so often to mine.

I realized I was staring at them when Robin turned back to me. "Let's go to my room," she said. She spoke quietly, not the way she does at school or at my house.

In her room, I said, "Your mom's a nice lady."

Robin was getting her shorts on, and she didn't look up, but she nodded. "Yeah, she is."

"Robin." I said it quickly, unsure if I should, never having done it before, but I wanted to know. "Robin, what's the matter with your mom? I mean, I know you told me once that she's depressed, but . . ."

"Shush!" Robin put a finger over her lips, and she glanced quickly at the door.

I looked, too, but no one was there, and Robin went to the door and very quietly closed it. "Do you know what agoraphobia is?" she said.

I shook my head. "I couldn't even *say* it."

"It means fear of open spaces, fear of going outside. That's what my mom's afraid of. Actually, she's afraid of lots of other things too, even people coming to the house. But she's getting better. I told you about her medicine,

84

and she's seeing a doctor.'' She paused, as though debating something, then added, ''She was really trying to see if she could go to the gymnastics show tonight. But I don't know if she will. It's so scary for her.''

''Wow! Really? You mean she's scared just to go out of the house?''

I must have sounded shocked, because Robin looked at me, annoyed. ''Yeah, and it's not her fault! Think how bad she must feel.''

''Oh, I know. I mean . . .'' I didn't, but I realized it was hard for Robin. Her life's always been so different from everyone else's. She's never been able to have anyone visit her, and her mom never attended any of the school events. ''Do you think she'll be there tonight?'' I asked.

Robin shrugged. ''I don't know. She seems more scared tonight than she has before, possibly just because she's thinking about it. But when my father comes home, maybe. Who knows?'' She shrugged, then smiled at me the way she usually did, with that half-laughing, half-teasing look. ''But we're going to be great, so it doesn't matter.''

''Yeah,'' I said. ''Yeah.'' But I knew it mattered to her a lot.

''Robin?'' It was Mrs. Harris, calling from the kitchen.

Robin opened the door quickly. ''Coming, Mom.''

Together, Robin and I went down the hall to the kitchen. A plate of cookies was on the table, as well as two mugs of hot chocolate. There were marshmallows floating in the cups, and steam was rising from them. I realized then how hungry I was. I had forgotten to eat! We smiled at each other and sat down. ''Thanks, Mom!'' Robin called. But Mrs. Harris wasn't in the kitchen, and she didn't answer.

CHAPTER
Fourteen

By the time Robin and I got back to school at six o'clock, the gym was open. I had a feeling that Robin knew something was wrong at my house, but she didn't ask and I didn't say anything. I was thankful, though, that she hadn't asked. It's always been that way with Robin and me. She seems to know when we can talk about things really personal and when not to ask.

In the gym we stripped off our sweatsuits and began doing warm-ups. I felt good, and my muscles were loose. Something was building inside me, a feeling that I wanted to do something dramatic, really show-offy. Why I wanted to do it, I wasn't sure, but I did. I thought about chinning off the bar the way Robin had done that day and wondered again if she had forgotten it.

We finished our warm-ups and began rehearsing the rope routine. When we were way up near the ceiling, I looked at Robin. "Robin," I asked, "are you going to chin off the bar the way you did that other time?"

Robin laughed. "Funny you thought about that right now. I was thinking the same thing."

"Going to do it?"

Robin paused for a minute. "Depends."

"On what?"

"Don't know. Things."

"Like what?"

"Just things. Don't bug me."

I looked at her, surprised. Robin never tells me to mind my own business. "Sorry," I said, just a little sarcastically. "Don't be so touchy."

"Well, I just don't know, that's all." She looked away and up at the bar. "Just depends."

And just like that, I knew what it depended on. It depended on whether or not her mother was there, but I didn't know whether she was going to do it if her mother *was* there or if her mother wasn't there. I also knew I shouldn't ask.

We shimmied down the ropes then and ran to get the mats for our floor routines. Neither of us spoke for a few minutes while we tugged the mats into place. All the time I was wondering what I could do that would be dramatic, that would really show off. If it couldn't be chinning off the bar, it had to be something else, maybe a forward midair flip. I had never done it before—Robin and I were each going to do a backward one in our floor routine— and I didn't think I could learn it that fast. In a forward flip, you have to get really high off the floor, almost as high as you can get by springing on a trampoline. The trampoline! That was it! I wasn't scheduled for the trampoline, but I bet I could do it. I looked over. It was set up in the other part of the gym, across from where the ropes were. Maybe after Robin and I finished our rope routine and just before we were to climb down, if I swung my rope really far out, I could drop on the trampoline? I

tried to measure with my eyes. I thought I could reach.
Maybe. I'd have to check.

"Oh, Sarah?"

Robin was standing on the mat, watching me, waiting
for me.

"Oh, hey," I said. "I'm sorry." I bent and did the
first rollover of our routine. "I was thinking."

"About what?" Robin asked.

I grinned at her from my upside down position. "Something."

She grinned back. "We have lots of secrets tonight,
don't we?"

I laughed, but I didn't feel good about it. We worked
hard then, practicing our routines over and over. We didn't
need much practice because we were as perfect as two
people can be with our routine. I know that sounds stuck-
up, but it was true. After we had practiced for a while,
some of the other kids began arriving, and even some of
the parents. Since most of the gym was filled with gymnastics
equipment, there was space for only a few rows of chairs
around the edges. Most of the parents would have to stand,
so a lot of them were getting there early. I took a quick
look at the arriving parents, just in case Mom and Daddy
were there, but they weren't. Thinking about them, watching
the other parents come in, I felt a lump in my throat and
swallowed hard. But I didn't begin to cry.

Robin and I went to the lavatory then to wash up and
get ready. Standing in front of the mirror and combing my
hair, I saw Robin watching me, and I smiled. We don't
look at all alike. I'm kind of tall and blonde, and she's
little and dark, but we did look really good dressed alike

in our red-and-white outfits. We both had our hair done the same way, too, pinned up at the sides with the back hanging loose. It would have been better to have it in a ponytail, but then the knot on the back of the head would get in the way when we did backward rollovers. Robin smiled at me in the mirror. "Ready?"

"Ready."

We went out to the gym and took our places with the rest of the kids. There was a special section set up for participants, and we all sat down together. There was also a special place for little kids because a kindergarten class had been invited to do the first part of the show. I guess they didn't have a big enough gym in their own school. I took one more quick look for Mom and Daddy and for Robin's parents too, but I didn't see any of them.

At exactly seven-thirty, Mr. Anderson went to the front of the gym and made his speech about how hard we had worked and all that, and then there was a song and the show began. The little kids went first, and they were fun to watch. There was one tiny one, and she was great on the balance beam. Everybody cheered her, and then, for some reason, she broke into tears. Then people cheered her even more, and eventually she smiled and finished her routine. Robin and I smiled at each other.

Our class came next, and then it was almost time for Robin and me. We exchanged looks, and suddenly, even though I knew we were as perfect as we could be, I started to get nervous. What if we made a mistake? What about the trampoline? What about Mom and Daddy—had they come in while I was sitting there? I wanted to turn and look for them, but I didn't because maybe they weren't there. I wondered about Robin's mom too, and I noticed Robin twisting around every so often, but I didn't ask if she had seen her.

Finally, when Julia began her routine, Robin and I knew it was our turn next. We went up and took our places out front, ready to go on. I saw Robin glance once more over the crowd, but I didn't look anywhere except at Julia. When she did the rollover that marked the end of her routine, my stomach felt like a knot in my middle. I looked at Robin, but she seemed cool, and that helped. I took a deep breath.

People applauded Julia, and then Robin and I ran out on the mat. We had rehearsed everything, even the way we would run out: hand in hand, then doing a twisting handspring in the center of the mat. As we did it, I heard the audience suck in their breaths, and we got instant, spontaneous applause. Robin grinned and winked at me. I was definitely less nervous. We ran to the ropes then. Up like a pair of monkeys, swing hard, exchange ropes. We had done it so often for so many months that I didn't even have to think. Flip over, hang down, dangling by our legs held tight around the ropes. Swing upside down, reach over, clasp hands. The audience was applauding at each new thing, but I heard it only dimly. Robin and I had our eyes glued to each other, marking each move, each bit of timing. We straightened up finally, marking the end of our rope routine. The floor routine was next, but first the descent. I paused for just an instant. Would Robin swing out over the bar, that slippery metal bar that supported the ropes? Should I try the trampoline descent? How far was it? I was aware that Robin had paused too, that even the audience was silent. I looked at Robin, then looked down. Every eye in the place was turned up, watching us, Daddy smiling, Mom biting her lip. Mom! Daddy! Mom was in a wheelchair near the back door, a wheelchair! But she was there. I looked at Robin. She reached out and took my hand. We had never done this before, but together we shimmied down, holding hands.

I knew there were tears in my eyes, but happy tears, sad tears, it didn't matter. I blinked them away fast. "Oh, please, please, let Robin's mom be here, please!" I prayed silently.

On the mat, we swung into our routine, fast, smooth. First the backward walkover, then the two-person roll, leaping over and over each other, as in leapfrog. That brought loud applause. Splits, cartwheels, two-handed walkovers, and then our finale—the midair backward flips. First mine, Robin standing close by, hands out to support my back if I fell. But I didn't. And then hers, me spotting her for safety. Perfect. We swept to one knee, hands clasped, in a deep bow. The audience roared. And then they all stood up, and for the first time, Robin and I lost our cool. Neither of us had expected a standing ovation. We looked at each other, and I could see tears forming in Robin's eyes and feel them in my own. We both smiled at everybody and whispered, "Thank you." And then we ran off the floor and fled to the lavatory.

Fifteen

✎ "SHE'S THERE!" Robin exclaimed when we got into the lavatory.

"I know," I answered, wiping tears from my eyes, feeling stupid for crying.

"My father was holding her hand tight, and she looked terrified. But she was there!"

For a second I was confused. *Her* father was holding my mother's hand? I looked at Robin, and she was wiping away tears, too, and then I realized what she meant. Her mother was out there! Her mother and my mother. And both of our fathers.

We looked at each other in the mirror then, both of us scrubbing away tears, and then we began to laugh. We laughed so hard that we had to lean back against the wall to catch our breaths. "Now, are we stupid or are we stupid?" I asked at last when we had recovered enough to speak. "Crying because we're happy!"

"Yeah." Robin took a deep, shaky breath. "Imagine what we'd be like if we were sad."

That started both of us laughing again helplessly, but after a while we stopped, although we both giggled again every once in a while. Then we washed our faces and smoothed our hair. Robin bent way over, flipped her hair up over her head, and ran her fingers through it. While she was bent over like that, she said, "Why's your mom in a wheelchair?"

I looked at her, but couldn't see her face. "You saw her?" I said slowly.

"Yeah. What's the matter with her?"

"I don't know," I answered. It was all I could say. I didn't know and couldn't have talked about it even if I did.

"Something happened today, didn't it?" Robin stood up then, flipped her hair back into place, but still she didn't look at me. "I could tell when you came to my house before."

I just shrugged. Robin looked at me in the mirror then. "It'll be okay, Sarah. You wait and see."

"Yeah, I hope. Let's go watch the rest of the show."

We went back to the gym, but I couldn't pay much attention to the other kids because I kept watching Mom. From where I sat, she looked okay, although it was weird to see her in that wheelchair. Where had she been? Obviously, something had gone wrong. She must have been sick again, maybe at the hospital, or she'd never have come here in a wheelchair. But why?

She and Daddy seemed happy, though. They kept whispering to each other, pointing out things that the gymnasts were doing, and they seemed pleased with everything they saw.

As soon as the show was over, I ran to them by the back door and threw my arms around Mom, not even caring who saw me or what anybody thought. I was so glad to see her! Also, I felt, in my mind at least, I had to make up to her for being so angry at her before.

She held me close and ran her hands through my hair. "You were wonderful," she whispered. "Just wonderful!"

I straightened up and looked at her. She looked dreadful, hardly any color at all, and even the whites of her eyes were yellowish. But she was smiling at me, and the smile was the same as it had always been. "I was scared," she added softly.

"About what? You know I've been practicing that for ages."

Mom nodded. "But there was something more, something about what you were going to do at the end of the rope routine." She looked at me questioningly.

How could she have known? I turned away without answering.

Mom pulled me close again. "It's been so hard for you," she said. "I'm sorry I wasn't there this afternoon. We called you and called you."

"Where were you?"

"At the hospital. They said I needed blood, a transfusion, right away."

"Blood! Why?" I looked at her, amazed, but before she could answer, people began crowding around us. Some of them were trying to get through the door that we were partly blocking. Some of them were trying to talk to Mom, friends who wanted to know, same as me, what she was doing in that wheelchair.

Daddy bent over Mom then. "Suppose we get out of here," he said quietly. "We can talk better at home."

Mom smiled at him. "In just a minute." She turned

94

to me. "Where's Robin? I want to congratulate her. She was wonderful too."

I turned and stood on tiptoe, trying to look over the crowd to see if I could see her. But there was such a mob, I couldn't single out Robin or her parents. Knowing about her mom though, I thought they had probably left right away. "I think she's gone," I told Mom. "I think they left right away, but maybe you can call her later."

Mom nodded and stood then, pushing herself up by the arms of the chair. Daddy reached for her, but she put one hand gently against his chest, pushing him away. "No," she said. "Let me. I'm not going out of here in this." She made a face at the wheelchair, then winked at me. But I wanted her to sit back down. She didn't look strong enough to walk, much less fight the mob that was pushing toward the door.

I took her arm and realized with a shock how thin she was. Her arm was just a bone, and her elbow, a ridge of knobs. "Are you okay, Mom?" I asked, and immediately wished I hadn't.

Mom nodded slightly. "I'll do," she said.

Outside, Daddy led us to the car, folded the wheelchair, and put it in back. Mom held my arm tightly, leaning on me so hard that she was almost hurting me, but she smiled at friends, shrugging when they asked what was the matter. "Just a little sick," was all she said to anyone.

In the car, no one said much, and Mom leaned her head back against the seat, panting as though she had been running.

At home, Daddy left the wheelchair in the car, and the three of us went up the walk together. Mom was between

Daddy and me, leaning on both of us for support, the way she had done that first time she came home from the hospital. But this time, she didn't say anything about how good it was to be back. It seemed that it was taking all of her energy just to get to the house.

In the front hall, Daddy and I helped her take off her coat, and she was still panting, that funny, gasping way. She looked at me once and rolled her eyes and shook her head, as though laughing at herself, but she didn't speak. She just nodded in the direction of the morning room.

Daddy practically carried her there and helped her into a chair, where she sank down, exhausted, her eyes closed.

My heart was racing as though I had been running, too. What was it? What was wrong? How could it happen so fast? She had been so good two nights ago, the night of the party! I held my breath, waiting for her to say something, and I warned myself not to cry, not to let her open her eyes and see me crying. But I needn't have worried because she didn't open her eyes for a very long time.

Daddy stood over her, his eyes glued to her face. "Honey?" he said softly after a while.

"Mmm?" she said. But I couldn't tell if she was answering him or if it was a little moan of pain.

"Honey," Daddy said, leaning close to her. "Honey, don't you think you'd be better off in the hospital?"

Mom shook her head.

"But remember what the doctor said?" Dad put a hand on her forehead, stroking it softly. "He said he could help with the pain?"

Again, Mom shook her head, still with her eyes closed.

I could see a pulse beating in her temple, throbbing fast, and her breath was coming in rapid little spurts. Neither of them seemed to notice that I was there. It was as if I were all alone in that room.

I began to cry, but quietly. What was the matter with my mother? Why did she look like that? Why didn't she talk to me, say something, anything?

As though she had read my mind, she opened her eyes then and looked at me. "Come here, love," she whispered. She motioned to me just a little.

I went to her, but stood a little distance away, afraid. But she motioned me closer and patted her lap. I went to her, kneeled down, and put my head in her lap, but I didn't sit there because I knew she couldn't hold me. When I put my head on her bony knees, I began to sob out loud. I didn't know it would be like this! I didn't know. I couldn't speak, but thoughts were clear in my head: My mother was dying, and I was crying so hard that I felt as if I would die too.

After a long time, Mom lifted up my head. "Hey," she said. "You've got to stop now. Got to."

But I just shook my head, and although I didn't put it in her lap again, I kept right on crying.

"Don't worry," Mom whispered.

I shrugged because I knew she didn't mean it.

She began crying, too. "I wish . . ." She broke off.

Again I only nodded.

"I love you so much," Mom said, and she put a hand on my face, and then reached up to Daddy with her other hand.

Daddy held it, and for a while none of us said anything.

But then Mom took a deep, trembly breath. "I feel a little better," she said quietly. "Think you could help me upstairs to bed?"

Daddy nodded and leaned over her. I backed away, making room for him, but he didn't help Mom to her feet. Instead, he lifted her up in his arms, and she let him, leaning against him as though she were a baby. She smiled at me. "Come on," she whispered. "Upstairs, all of us. A good night's sleep and we'll feel better."

I nodded, but I didn't say anything. She was right, though. We had to go to bed.

CHAPTER
Sixteen

🖋 CHRISTMAS EVE MORNING. It was as silent in the house as though everybody were dead. Dead. The word didn't do anything to me any more, didn't make my heart race the way it used to. I lay on my back in bed, staring at the ceiling. I had Christmas presents for Mom, and for Daddy, and for Robin. They were already wrapped and in a stack at the foot of the bed. I had bought two little blue angels for Mom, tiny china angels with candles in their hands. Were there really such things as angels?

I couldn't stay in bed, so I got up, put on my robe, and tiptoed down the hall to Mom and Daddy's room. I didn't even knock but just opened the door and peeked in.

They were still in bed, Daddy lying on his side, his mouth open, snoring slightly. Mom was beside him, propped up on several pillows, but she was awake and she smiled at me when I opened the door. She put one finger over her lips and whispered, "I'll get up and meet you downstairs. Let's let Daddy sleep."

I nodded, watching as Mom slowly got out of bed and reached to the chair alongside for her robe. She seemed better this morning, as though it wasn't such an effort for her to move, but I could hardly believe how skinny she was under her nightgown. She looked over her shoulder, saw me watching her, and smiled. "I'm fine!" she whispered. She went into the bathroom then and closed the door.

I went down to the kitchen, where I started the coffee. I was a lot better at it than I had been that first time when Mom came home from the hospital, and I was pleased when it dripped into the pot, nice and dark brown. It was just finished when Mom arrived in the kitchen. She walked a little unsteadily, trailing one hand along the wall as though to keep her balance, but she smiled at me. "Mmm, coffee's ready. You're terrific."

I smiled back and got a mug, poured the coffee, and took it to her. She sat at the table, seeming satisfied to let me wait on her, but even as she sat there, she was breathing hard.

"How do you feel?" I asked.

"Better than last night." Mom sighed softly. "Yes, better than last night."

My heart did a little flip.

"That was a tough night."

"What happened?" I asked, almost against my will.

"The cancer's invaded my bones, my liver," Mom answered. "It's causing the pain I'm having, and the jaundice too—the thing that's making me look so yellow. It's a little complicated—I'm not sure I understand it myself—but that's why I needed blood right away." It was as if she were talking about a soccer game, just as calm, just as normal. She sighed, closing her eyes and leaning her head back against the chair. When she opened her eyes, she smiled at me. "But I'm home, Sarah. Home for Christmas. And I'm staying here."

I nodded, but I didn't ask anything because I didn't want to know anything more.

Mom set her cup on the table and leaned close to me. "Sarah, stop looking at me as though I were going to explode. I'm not, you know. This is bad, I know. It's not good. But it's Christmas Eve." She put a finger up to my face. "I order you to enjoy it."

I couldn't help smiling at her, and I raised one hand to my forehead in a pretend salute. "Yes, ma'am!"

"That's better." Mom smiled at me, too. "Now, some unfinished business. What were you planning to do last night when you were at the top of the ropes?"

I picked up a paper napkin and folded it carefully, turning all the corners toward the middle. "Nothing, really."

"Sarah, look at me. Answer me."

I looked at her and took a deep breath. "Nothing much. I was just— Well, I was going to try to drop onto the trampoline."

Mom's eyes opened wide with surprise. "You *what*! Why?"

"Why? I don't know. Just because."

Mom took a deep breath and let it out slowly. "Sarah, think about it, about why you wanted to do that. Wasn't it enough . . ." She paused, then repeated it insistently, "Wasn't it *enough* to do all those daring things you've been practicing?"

I shrugged. "No, it wasn't. I mean— Well, it was— once I saw you there." I was confused, not sure myself if I knew what I was talking about.

But Mom seemed to understand something I didn't and

it seemed to worry her. "Sarah," she said, "sometimes when we're troubled or worried or disappointed, we do things we shouldn't do, wild things." She nodded as though agreeing with herself. "It's as though we were tempting the Fates. It's a form of running away, thinking it's easier to face the dangers outside than the ones we feel threatened by inside. Do you know what I mean?"

I didn't answer. I wasn't quite sure, but I did know that I had never wanted to do anything like that except last night. I also knew that it had been easier to think about that than to think about Mom and what might be happening.

Mom continued, and she was breathing hard again, almost gasping. "It's been so hard for you, being worried about me. So maybe you were running a little. I've often worried about Robin and the wild things she does—as though she were running from something."

"But she didn't do anything wild last night. Mom, guess what?"

"What?" Mom leaned close, and I realized it had been so long since we had talked like this about my friends and how I felt, anything except about her being sick.

"Robin's mom has been sick with some disease I can't remember the name of, but it makes her too scared to leave the house. And you know what? Last night she went out, the first time in years that she went to school. She was at the gymnastics show!"

"That's wonderful! Robin must have been so happy."

I nodded. "Yeah, and she was going to chin off the bar up there, and it's really dangerous, but she didn't do it."

"Because her mother was there?"

I shrugged. I wondered about that. Maybe. I only knew that Robin had been happier last night than I've ever known her to be.

Mom put one hand on my cheek. It felt hot against my face, and I looked at her quickly to see if she was feverish, but her face wasn't flushed, and she was smiling at me. "Don't be wild," she said. "Dare a lot, but don't be wild."

I nodded.

"Promise?" She sounded much more serious than she looked.

"I promise," I said, and Mom let out her breath as though she were relieved.

"Now, go get Daddy," Mom said, "and let's get on with the business of Christmas. We need a good Christmas Eve breakfast, and he's the one to make it."

I ran up the stairs to their room, knocking that time. It took him only a few minutes to get ready, and in no time at all he was in the kitchen starting to cook the sausages and French toast.

We have lots of traditions at Christmas, and one of them is what we eat for Christmas Eve breakfast. It always has to be sausages, no matter what else we have with them, because when I was little, I used to love sausages. Now I hate them, but on Christmas Eve I eat them. We have lots of other traditions too, things that we do just the way we did them when I was little—like the way we get our presents. We open them all—all but two—on Christmas morning, and they don't even go under the tree till then because when I was little, Santa didn't bring them until after I was in bed. We get two presents on Christmas Eve

103

as soon as it gets dark. That's because when I was little, Mom said I was too excited to wait for Christmas morning.

Now, while Daddy made breakfast, I set the table and Mom sat there talking to us. Out of the corner of my eye, I kept watching her, and I thought she looked a little better. Her color was better, and her eyes were bright and shining, like the pictures taken of me in front of the Christmas tree, the tree lights reflected in my eyes, when I was little. She was laughing a lot too, at the silly things that Daddy and I were saying. We were trying to remember every single present we had gotten for Christmas in the past thirteen years, ever since I was born. I wasn't too good at remembering the years I was one and two years old, but I was better after that. Daddy was hopeless. He kept mentioning things that Mom had given him, and he'd describe them in detail, and then Mom would tell him that they were presents he had gotten from Grandma, not from her. Or else he'd describe something he thought I had given him when I was four, but it was really when I was nine. He kept getting everything all mixed up.

When we finally sat down to breakfast, we were all laughing—Mom, too, although she had a funny, faraway look in her eyes, as though she were remembering those other Christmases.

CHAPTER
Seventeen

✍ WE ATE QUIETLY for a while, I guess each of us remembering. Then Mom looked at me and asked, in that sort of breathless way, "What was . . . your favorite . . . Christmas?"

"Hmm, I don't know. They've all been so good." I put down my fork, thinking. "Maybe the year I got Sleepyhead. Remember Sleepyhead?"

Mom smiled. "Of course."

Daddy smiled, too. "How could we forget? You dragged her everywhere for two years."

I laughed because I *had* done that. She was my favorite doll, a big, soft thing, like a stuffed animal. Her face was round and sweet, but her eyes didn't open, and that's how she got her name—Sleepyhead. I have her still, although I don't play with her any more. But she's up there in my room, on top of my bookcase.

"What made that your favorite Christmas?" Daddy asked. "Do you know?"

"Yup, because when I went to see Santa that year, for some reason, I was afraid of him. Remember, the doll came in two sizes, a big one and a little one? Well, because I was scared, I was afraid to ask for the big one, so I just asked—I whispered, I remember it—for the little one. And then for weeks I prayed that Santa would know it was the big one I wanted." I smiled at Mom and Daddy. "And of course Santa knew, and I got the big one. Santa always knew what I wanted in those days."

"Does he still know?" Mom asked.

I laughed. "I guess so. I've never been disappointed."

"What do you hope for this year?" Mom asked. "Even though it's too late to do anything about it." She paused, panting again. "What do you hope for?"

I shrugged, unable to answer. I had been hoping for a stereo but I knew they cost a lot, and although I had hinted, I hadn't asked outright. Usually I ask for what I want, but with Mom sick and in the hospital so much, I was afraid it was too expensive. But I didn't much care what I got. Everything Mom and Daddy picked out for me was always good.

"Come on," Mom teased. "Tell us one little thing you want."

"For you to get better soon." I blurted it out. I hadn't meant to say that, but it just came out.

Daddy nodded hard, but Mom seemed to dismiss my answer. "What else?" she said, laughing, and she looked at me in that teasing way she had, and for an instant, she looked almost the way she used to. "Come on, tell."

"A cat," I answered, surprising myself. "A kitten." I hadn't even thought of that before, but thinking about Sleepyhead, remembering how she felt, I suddenly wanted something to hold. And I was way too big for dolls.

"A kitten?" Mom sounded as surprised as I was. "Hmm, they're hard to find on Christmas Eve." She looked at

Daddy. "Think Santa . . . has any . . . Christmas Eve specials . . . on kittens?"

Daddy looked worried. "Well, I don't know. . . ."

I couldn't believe they were taking me seriously! I've always wanted a pet, but Mom has so many allergies, I've never been allowed to have one except hamsters or things that have to stay in a cage. "Are you serious?" I asked. "Could I really have a kitten?"

"Well, I don't know if we could find one today," Mom breathed. "Christmas Eve and all. But after today. Why not?"

"But your allergies!"

Mom just smiled.

"No," I said, "definitely not. It would bother your allergies too much." I would not think about why I might be allowed to have a pet now. "Come on," I said, standing up. "We still have Christmas Eve things to do. We have to decorate the cookies."

Daddy stood up too, and we both began clearing the table. Slowly Mom got up and went toward the stairs to go get dressed. I watched her go, using her hand to steady herself against the wall again. When she got to the stairs, she stopped and rested on each step.

After Daddy and I had done the dishes, I went up to get dressed too. I put on my favorite jeans and sweater and my Christmas socks, the red ones with the green Christmas trees on them. The socks are really small now because Mom bought them for me years ago, but they've become a tradition too.

When I was dressed, I went down to the kitchen. Neither Mom nor Daddy was down yet, so while I waited, I got out the cookies and the icing things. It took Mom a long time, and when she finally came down, she was all dressed, and had make-up on, too. I couldn't help thinking that it didn't do much good. Her color was awful, but the worst part was the way she breathed, seeming to get out of breath at every little thing, even from talking. So she sat down at the table, but that was all right because you can decorate cookies better sitting down, anyway. To decorate, we use colored sugar icing thinned with water, and we put it on the cookies with tiny paint brushes. We did Santas and trees and angels, and I loved it. Why had I ever given up painting in those paint books I used to have? Painting was fun!

When we finished, Mom went back upstairs. She said she was going to wrap more presents, but I was pretty sure she was going to take a nap. I didn't care, though, because I still had more presents to wrap, so I didn't mind being alone.

It was about three o'clock, and I was in my room with the door closed, just putting the tape on the Arnolds' present, when Daddy knocked. "Punkin?" he called.

"Come in," I answered.

He opened the door a little. "Come on down to the morning room, would you?"

"Sure. Why?" But he was already gone, so I finished putting the ribbon on and went down.

Mom and Daddy were both in the morning room, sitting together on the sofa. Under the tree was a ton of presents. But they've never put the presents out till I was asleep at night! "What's this for?" I asked angrily. They had no right to change traditions!

There was a little silence, and then Daddy said, "We thought you might like to exchange presents now."

"What! We can't do that. It's not Christmas yet!"

Daddy took a deep breath. "We wanted to see you open them."

"Dad-dy! Stop it. It's not Christmas."

I looked at Mom. She always sides with me, but she wasn't saying anything now, not even looking at me. She sat straight and very stiffly, almost holding her breath, and her hands were clenched as though she were holding onto something invisible.

"Mom?"

"What?" she whispered.

"Mom, why are we doing this?"

"I don't know," she said, so quietly that I could barely hear her, and she was panting. "We thought . . . you'd like . . . to have your presents."

"Well, I wouldn't!"

She looked at me then, and her eyes were bright. "All right," she gasped. "How about our two gifts? The ones . . . we exchange . . . at night?"

"But it's not night yet, either!"

"Sarah, please?" Daddy said.

"All right." Just like that I said it, but I began to cry. I couldn't think about this, about what was happening. I ran up to my room and got their presents. The tennis shirt and tennis balls for Daddy. The two little china angels with the candles for Mom. I raced back down the stairs.

Daddy had moved to the arm of the sofa and was holding Mom tightly around the shoulders. But Mom looked even weirder, as though she weren't there any more. She was still sitting straight and stiff, still holding onto that something invisible, but now her eyes were wide, blank, and staring.

I went to them then, put their presents in their laps, and turned away, crying.

"Sarah?" Daddy called to me, and reached out to me. "Come here."

I didn't want to, didn't want to be near what was happening. Yet I turned and went.

As I did, Mom suddenly lifted both hands, pressed them hard against her forehead. She looked at me once, her eyes huge, and for an instant, it was as if she were pleading with me.

"What?" I cried.

She took her hands away from her forehead then, held them out to me, still asking, but she didn't speak. Then she began rolling her head back and forth, harder and faster, and her eyes did something funny, twitched, and her mouth did, too. Then one hand flew up, and she gripped Daddy's arm hard, and her head fell back against the sofa.

I screamed. Somebody screamed. I put my hands over my ears, but the sound went on. I flew up the stairs to my room, slammed the door, and fell face down on my bed, burying my head in the pillow.

It was quiet then downstairs, quiet everywhere. The screaming had stopped. Quiet for a very long time. I don't know how long I was there, maybe a long time, nothing happening inside me. Then sounds came up from downstairs, soft sounds of people coming and going. After a while— how long?—Daddy came in without even knocking, came right over to the bed, picked me up, and held me close. "Sarah, you know Mom's dead. You know."

I nodded.

"Do you want to come downstairs and . . . see her? I've called the funeral home. Someone will be here in a while."

"*See her*?" I cried. "She's dead, isn't she?"

Daddy didn't answer, but he pulled me closer, and we stood together, him holding me tightly, my ribs hurting from the pressure of his arms. The doorbell rang, and then rang again. I heard a voice, as someone went to answer it. "Who's downstairs?" I asked.

"The Arnolds. I called. They came right away."

"Why did she die?"

Daddy didn't answer.

"*Why*?" I really meant it, really didn't know. Mothers didn't die. Not *mothers*!

"I don't know, Sarah." Daddy was crying, too, but he sounded almost angry, and I knew I shouldn't be asking him things like this now. But I was lonely, and scared too. Scared because Mom had wanted something from me when she held out her hands to me. I didn't know what it was. I didn't give it to her. And that made me cry harder. What did she want?

"Come downstairs, please?" Daddy said.

I nodded, and he took my hand as though I were a little child, and together we went down the stairs. I didn't want to see Mom then, dead. I did not want to see her. Yet a part of me wanted to see her very much.

I went into the morning room with Daddy. The Arnolds

were there, and Mom too. She was lying on the sofa covered up with a blanket up to her chin, just as if she were sleeping. She looked just the way she always does when she sleeps, too, quiet, but awfully still. Out of the corner of my eyes, I could see the Arnolds leave the room. There were so many tears—something in my throat too—so I felt like choking or throwing up. I whispered to her, "Mommy." I kneeled down beside the sofa, wanting to throw myself into her lap, into her arms, the way I had the night before. But instead, I just put a hand on her hair, and it was soft, and I realized I hadn't touched her hair in so long. Then I whispered something to her, something stupid. I whispered, "Good-bye."

I stood up then and turned to Daddy. "What did she want before when she looked at me like that? I don't know!"

"To live." Daddy was crying. "To see you grow up."

"But I couldn't give it to her, and she died!"

"It's not your fault. None of us could make her better. But she did want you to know something."

"What?" We were both crying so hard that I could barely see him, and I don't think he could see me, either. But he held something out to me.

It was a small package, wrapped in shiny silver Christmas paper and tied with red ribbon and a bow.

"What is it?"

"It's from Mom. She's been writing it for you. It's a letter. Maybe you'd even call it a book. Things she wanted you to know. She started it a long time ago. She wrote the last thing in it this morning."

I took it and tore it open. What did she say? What did

she want? It was a book, one of those blank books you can buy, and she had written in it, filled it, almost, with her writing. I looked at the first page, but then flipped through quickly to the last—to the last thing she had wanted me to know.

CHAPTER
Eighteen

🖋 I AM LYING ON MY BED, and it's almost dark now. I am in the house alone, as I have been every afternoon for the past three months when I come home from school—alone except for Flicker and for Feisty, my cat, who's curled on the bed beside me. I am reading again the book from Mom and listening to my favorite record on my stereo. The book is getting worn out from my reading it so much, and I have memorized parts of it. Some make me happy, and some make me sad. There are pages where Mom jokes with me, and those parts make me saddest. I never knew I would miss her so much. It's funny, though, it's been a whole week since I've taken the book out, and I used to read it every day.

I'm doing something else now, and Mom would be surprised if she knew. I am keeping a notebook of my own. It's a thick spiral notebook that I bought with some of my Christmas money. In it, I write everything I do each day, and everything I think, sort of keeping track of things. When I learn something new, I write it down—like I've learned to do the laundry, and I'm not a bad cook at all. I'm even reading some of the books Mom bought for me, some of those grown-up authors she wanted me to know.

114

But the most important parts are the feelings. I'm doing that because of what Mom wrote to me those last two days she wrote in this book, the day of the gymnastics show, and Christmas Eve day.

I always used to turn to that part of the book first, so that now I have it memorized and hardly even have to look at it. On the day of the gymnastics show, she wrote this, and I can almost hear her saying it in that breathless way she had. "Sarah, today is the saddest day of your young life. The hardest and most important thing that anyone must do is to let go. When I am gone, you must let go of me. Not stop loving me. Not stop remembering me. But keep what I've given you. Keep what's important to you, and let go of the rest. And go on. You have Daddy to love and care for. And Grandma and Grandpa. And Robin, and even her mom. And the Arnolds. And so much. But most of all, you have yourself. Maybe, because of what is happening to you, you will always be lonely in some small corner of your heart and soul. Don't run from that. It will make you tender. And strong. Sarah, I love you so much, and that love will always be in your heart. So, I'm not completely gone, am I?"

That part used to make me really angry. "Yes, you're gone," I wanted to yell at her. "Being in my heart doesn't make me less lonely. I want to *see* you!" That's why I started writing, sort of as if I were writing to her, telling her how mad I am, and everything else I've been feeling. Funny, though, lately I don't feel I'm writing it for her so much. I almost feel as though I'm writing it for my own kids, although I don't know that I'll ever marry and have kids. But writing helps because it helps me understand

115

things. Yesterday, Robin told me her mother has been sick again and hasn't gone out of the house for a week. I told Robin that it's all right. See, you don't get all better suddenly. It's a little better, and then a little worse, like that game of giant steps we use to play—a big step forward, a little step back. So I know she'll get better again. Like me. Some days I cry all the time. Other days hours go by and I don't even think of Mom. That made me feel guilty at first. But I'm getting used to it a little, and Daddy says he sometimes feels the same way too.

It's weird with Daddy now. We share so much more than we used to, and that made me feel guilty for a while too, as if I wasn't being loyal to Mom because she and I used to share all those things. But I guess it's all right, and I guess Mom wouldn't mind because she did tell me to love and care for Daddy . . .

The phone just rang, and it was Robin. She's coming over, and together we're going to make dinner for us and Daddy. We've done that a couple of times, and it's fun. She said she got a seed catalogue, too, and she's bringing that over. We're planning to fix up the garden in the spring, so it will be pretty outside the morning room, just the way Mom planned it. At first I thought I was doing the garden for Mom, but now I'm not sure who I'm doing it for. Maybe for Daddy. Maybe for me.

I know one thing for sure, though. I know it because Mom wrote it, the last thing before she died. I know it because she's right. Of all the things that have been said since she died, it's the one thing that has helped. It was on the last page, and it's the only thing she dated. She put a time on it, too: 1:00, December 24. "Sarah," she wrote.

"Don't let anybody tell you differently. What we're going through stinks. It just plain stinks."

I think anyone else who saw that would laugh. But I know what she means, and she's right. I know I'm getting better. I know Daddy's going to get better. I know I'm growing up and learning a lot of things. And spring is coming, and I know I'm going to plant a garden. But I know something else. Mom is dead. And it stinks.

About the Author

Patricia Hermes was born in New York, where she received her B.A. from St. John's University. Besides YOU SHOULDN'T HAVE TO SAY GOOD-BYE, she has written three other books for young readers, and in addition has written articles for many magazines and newspapers including, *The New York Times*, *Life & Health*, and *Woman's Day*. Previously an English teacher at the high school level, Ms. Hermes has also conducted writing seminars for The Gifted and Talented Education program in the Norfolk, Virginia public schools.

She is married and the mother of five children and currently lives in Norfolk, Virginia.